# A LOVE OF BOOKS AND LEATHER

## ALEX CLIFFORD

# A LOVE OF BOOKS AND LEATHER

ALEX CLIFFORD

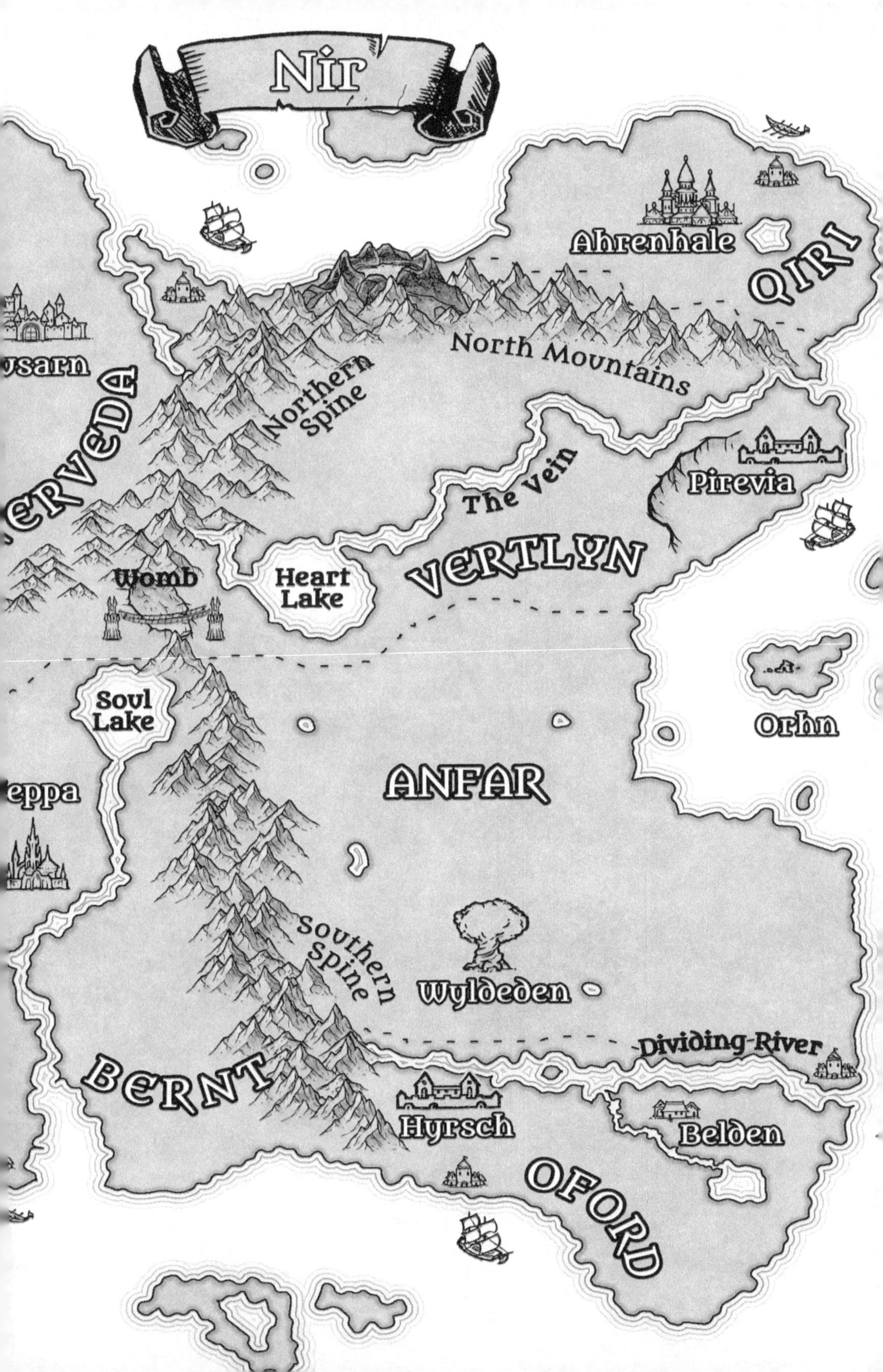

Nir
QIRI
Ahrenhale
North Mountains
Northern Spine
The Vein
Pirevia
VERTLYN
ysarn
ERVEDA
Womb
Heart Lake
Soul Lake
Orhn
ANFAR
eppa
Southern Spine
Wyldeden
Dividing River
BERNT
Hyrsch
Belden
OFORD

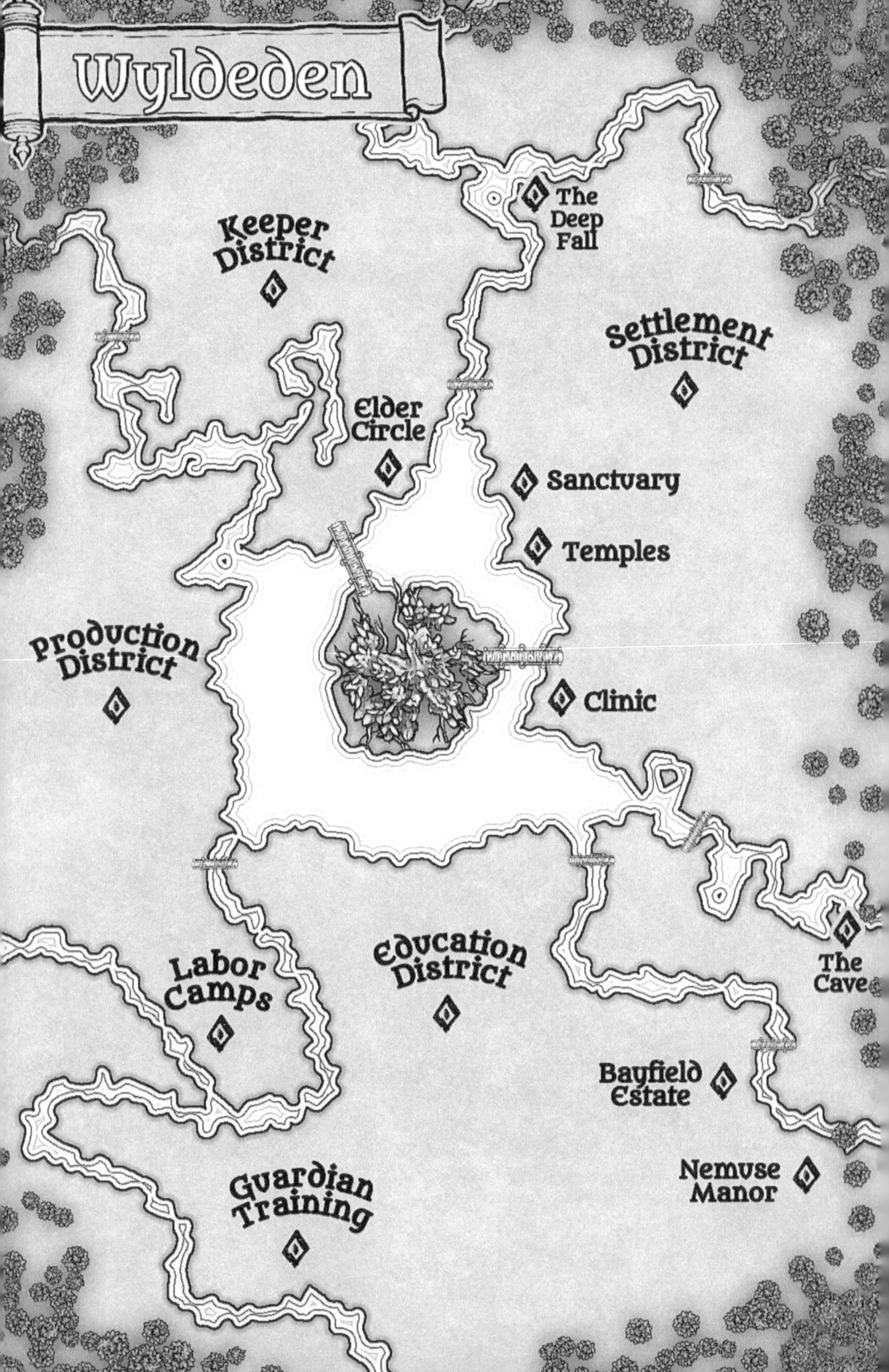

Wyldeden
Keeper District
The Deep Fall
Settlement District
Elder Circle
Sanctuary
Temples
Production District
Clinic
Labor Camps
Education District
The Cave
Bayfield Estate
Guardian Training
Nemuse Manor

# IN A PLACE ALL OUR OWN

CHAPTER I

# THE TEST

When Eaon's family had asked him how his qualifying tests were going, he had lied. With a smile on his face, he told everybody they were going well and conveniently found something more interesting to do or talk about before details could be asked for.

But now, there would be no more lying. Elementary school was coming to an end, the tests were done, and the scrap of parchment in his shaking fist would lay bare his failures for all to see.

He had not passed a single test of magic except to produce a whispering leaf—the absolute minimum to qualify as a witch at all. While all his friends had connected with the earth, the gardens and the flowers, Eaon had felt nothing. His da was from another clan, so they had tested for a proclivity toward other things like rock, crystal, and clay, but he still had not connected with anything.

*Recommended clan role: labor or travel.*

He had managed to accept the certificate without trembling, but as soon as he was alone he had broken down.

His parents were going to be heartbroken.

His Head of House was going to kill him.

In a dandelion field near the forest bordering Wyldeden sat a lichen-encrusted manor of stone. Eaon's parents had their own wing with a separate entrance, the kitchenette door wide open as one of the laborers employed by the Nemuse family carted a basket of dirty laundry to the nearby stream.

He didn't know her name. Had never bothered to learn it.

Quietly, he followed her to the stream and watched her kneel by the water. Taking out one of the tunics, she began to inspect it for stains.

"Excuse me," Eaon called.

The laborer gasped and spun round, clutching the tunic to her chest as her eyes widened. Then she bowed, forehead to the ground before him, as all the laborers Eaon had ever met had done. As he would learn to do.

It was as if he was seeing them for the first time. The shame of his blindness sank deep in his belly as this fully matured witch groveled to his lanky twelve-year-old self, as if he were a king in one of the human stories his da would read to him.

"What can I do for you, young one?"

"I . . . What is your name?"

The witch hesitated before she answered. "Have I offended you?"

"No." Eaon frowned, glancing back to the house. "Why would you think that?"

"That is why you wish to know my name, isn't it? So you can report me for some grievance? Whatever I have done, I am sorry. Please, don't—"

"No!" Eaon interrupted her, feeling sick as something akin to panic twisted his stomach. "Have I been rude to you before?"

"No, young one," she said, her head still down.

Eaon didn't know if he believed her. He couldn't remember ever being rude to the laborers, not the way many of his cousins were, but he wasn't sure he'd remember doing so if he had, either.

"I'm sorry," he said. "I'm sorry I bothered you."

He turned and rushed from the stream toward the open door of the kitchenette.

It would be another hour or so before his ma returned from her shift at the healer's clinic, but his da was sitting at the little table with a cup of tea and a map, planning his next adventure.

*Labor or travel.*

Perhaps he could travel like his da. See Nir for himself instead of just reading about it in stories.

"Eaon." Kailevi smiled at him and patted the seat beside him. "You look like you've seen a wraith."

Nervously, Eaon went to take the seat beside his da. "Are you leaving again soon?"

"In a week. You had your final tests today, didn't you? Are those your results?" Kailevi asked, nodding to the crumpled piece of paper in Eaon's hand.

Out of everyone, Eaon was least worried about what his da was going to say. He too had very little magic.

"Where's Eavha?" he asked, looking around for his younger sister. She was only eight, but already she had picked up some of the nasty habits of their cousins. He didn't want her to hear about his results before he'd had a chance to prepare.

"Playing with the neighbors." Kailevi's voice had gone quiet. As if he knew.

When Eaon still didn't hand over the parchment, Kailevi reached out and took it. Staring out the window as Kailevi unfolded the paper, Eaon winced at his da's sharp intake of breath.

"I'm sorry," Eaon managed, his voice breaking.

"No, I'm sorry. This is my fault."

"Eavha is so obviously blessed, so it can't be your fault."

"Well, it's certainly not yours." Kailevi took his son's jaw and moved his face until Eaon had no choice but to look up at him. "It's just how you were born."

Eaon said nothing. It made no difference where the blame was placed—in blood or character. Neither Terra, Sanni or any of the other Spirits had deemed him worthy of blessing, and that was all that mattered.

"It's going to be okay," Kailevi said again, pulling Eaon closer for a tight hug. "I promise you, everything will be okay."

There was a coven of sea witches who lived on the coast who liked to trade with the Wyldeden clan and had expressed a clear preference for dealing with Kailevi, so Eaon helped him plan his trip, outlining on a map of Nir the safest path through Anfar to the strait. Until voices drifted through the field, more of them filling the manor halls beyond the door to their wing. Then Eaon forgot how to breathe.

"Go to your room," Kailevi said softly. "I'll tell your ma."

"Is she going to be angry with me?"

"No. Of course not. I just think it best if I tell her. Go."

Kailevi shooed Eaon from the table, but he couldn't bear not knowing what his ma thought of him, so Eaon lingered in the hall with his ear toward the kitchen.

"Well, honey, it has been a day," his ma sighed as she came in. "Where are the kids?"

"Eavha will be back from the neighbors soon. Eaon is in his room."

"His tests?"

There was silence for a moment. Eaon knew she was reading the report when she started sobbing. Covering his face with his hands, he sank to the floor and buried his head in his knees.

"I prayed so hard," his ma cried.

"I know."

"It has to be a mistake."

"He's like me, Elly. We knew there was a chance he could be."

"We never should have taken the risk," she cried. "Maybe we could take him—"

"You know we can't. What's done is done. You and I will take care of him."

"We might not be enough."

"We will be."

*We never should have taken the risk.* The risk of having children when Kailevi was bringing low-blessed blood into the family. They resented him even being born.

Getting up, he ran to his room as quietly as he could.

---

At dinner, Eaon couldn't bring himself to eat. Any minute now the Head of House would remember him and ask how his final tests had gone. And he would have to tell the truth. In front of everyone.

Beneath the table, his ma took his hand and squeezed tightly.

He dared to look at her for the first time since she got home and, though her eyes were rimmed with red, she smiled.

The lump in his throat grew.

"Eaon," the Head turned to him.

"Dwys," his ma interupted. "Perhaps we can all talk in private after dinner."

The whispers began immediately. To request a private conversation about such a matter could only mean bad news.

"Eaon." The Head ignored her, his heavy gaze falling on Eaon. "What was your teacher's verdict today? Will you be joining us at the clinic? Or perhaps with some of the others in the fields?"

No matter how he swallowed, Eaon could not get the lump down his throat.

"No," he whispered.

"Dwys," his ma tried again.

"I am not speaking to you," the Head snapped without looking at her. He knew. He must. "Eaon will be starting secondary studies soon, it is time he learned to speak for himself. Share with us, Eaon, what will your clan role be?"

Eaon wished Eavha wasn't here. She was looking up at him with those big brown eyes, flowers braided in her hair. She was everything he had never been at her age, and while it was not her fault he was not blessed, he resented her all the same.

"Laborer or traveler," he said, shoulders bowing.

Silence settled across the table.

"Dwys," his ma said softly. Soothingly.

The Head slammed a hand down on the table. Everybody flinched.

"This is your fault for bringing in that foreign trash," he hissed at Eaon's ma. "It was one thing to marry Kailevi, but to give this family a Nemuse-blooded laborer is a disgrace!"

Eaon shut his eyes as the Head's tone became so sharp the crystal goblets on the table rattled.

His ma squeezed his hand tighter beneath the table.

The door slammed open and Eaon turned to see Kailevi storming in. He was not normally allowed to eat with them, but their own kitchen was close enough to the manor's enormous dining room that he had likely heard the shouting.

"You will not speak to her that way," Kailevi warned the Head.

A number of Eaon's unts and unks were trying to leave the table without being noticed. His cousins were shooting him dirty looks. They would never play together again.

In the corner, the laborer from the stream was watching. Eaon met her eye, but found no sympathy there.

"Get back in your own kitchen," the Head snapped, standing from his seat. "I should have petitioned to have you thrown from the Boab as soon as I realized she was falling for you. Now look at what your wasteful blood has done to our family line!"

Eaon flinched again as the Head pointed at him.

Eavha whimpered, running to their da to cling to his side. Kailevi tucked her behind him, but did not back down.

"This obsession with blessings is ridiculous. It changes nothing about how clever—"

"It changes everything!" The Head shouted, cracks splintering along the wood of the table where his hands rested. "He could be the cleverest witch in all of Wyldeden, but it means nothing if Terra and Sanni have not blessed him! He is unworthy to them, and thus worthless to us!"

"How dare you!" His ma stood, and the Head of House slammed his fists on the table again.

The wood cracked. Shattered.

Splinters flew through the room, and his ma wasn't quick enough to shove Eaon behind her to stop a few from nicking his face. More of them scratched her bare arms.

"How dare *you*, Ellissa," the Head spat. "How dare you."

His ma hissed, herding Eaon toward Kailevi. "Go to your da."

"Where do you think you're going?"

"I will not let you—"

"You have no authority here, Ellissa. Give him to me."

Eaon couldn't help the whine that came out of him as the Head came marching through the splinters toward them. Kailevi grabbed hold of Ellissa and tried to hide all three of them behind him.

Eaon wasn't exactly sure what happened next.

Someone pushed Eavha into his arms, and he shielded her as best he could as violence broke out behind him. But then a hand grabbed a fistful of his hair and pulled him away.

"No!" his ma cried from where she had fallen to the ground beside his da, a hand over a wound in his shoulder, healing magic churning the air thickly.

Eavha was sobbing, but he only heard it for a moment. A smack to the side of the head left his ear ringing, pain blossoming across his cheek.

"Stop cowering behind your parents like a worm. You have the blood of a laborer? So start laboring."

The Head shoved him to the ground among the broken pieces of table.

He didn't know what he was supposed to do but he remembered the way the laborer at the creek had bowed, so even though he was shaking, he copied her.

"Lower," the Head spat, placing a foot on the back of Eaon's head.

"Stop it!" his ma shouted.

"Get away from my son," Kailevi hissed then cried out in pain as he tried to get up.

Ellissa sobbed. "Get away from him, or I swear, I will petition to leave this family."

Eaon's cheekbone creaked against the floor as the Head shifted his weight.

"You can fuck off and live like the nameless then," he spat back. "You and your foreign husband and your useless child. But the talented one stays with me."

Eavha.

Eaon's fists clenched against the ground at the thought of his little sister here alone. His parents must have felt the same because they did not speak up again.

The pressure on his head lifted, and Eaon started to sit up. He only managed an inch before the foot slammed back down.

"Did I say you could rise?"

Eaon's eyes burned, but the next time the Head lifted his foot Eaon kept his head down.

The Head sneered at him. "Clean up this mess. If I find even one splinter in the rugs, I will jam it into your eye. Understood?"

"Yes," Eaon said quietly.

The Head stormed off, but Eaon didn't dare move. Neither did his family until the door to the dining room closed. Then Ellissa crawled to him and lifted his head off the floor.

"I'm so sorry. I'm so sorry," she cried, laying her palm on his bleeding cheek and beginning a prayer.

Kailevi scooped up Eavha, blood staining the front of his tunic as he joined Ellissa and Eaon on the floor. Healing magic warmed his face and turned his stomach, loosening the tears he'd been holding back.

"I'm going to figure something out. This will not be happening," Kailevi fumed.

But Eaon had paid attention in school. This was how things were. Nothing would change that, and unless they were willing to leave Eavha behind, Eaon would have to stay.

# CHAPTER 2
# THE BIRD

Dearmead whined as they marched along the path to the elementary school, his lanky legs struggling to keep up with his ma's long strides. He was twelve now, and bigger than most of the other males his age, but he still felt small under Calla's glare.

"You're holding back," she scolded, dragging him by the ear.

"Ow!"

"*Ow!*" she mocked him. "You think a rogue will care if you whinge at it? You think it will stop butchering your family if you shed a couple of tears? You're to be a guardian. Time to toughen up. Next time someone insults you, don't hold back. Understood?"

"Yes," Dearmead sulked.

They reached the elementary school and Calla let go of his ear, pushing him toward the gate. It wouldn't be long until he would start training at the secondary school where things would probably get harder. He wasn't looking forward to it.

"Good. Do not embarrass me," his ma hissed, then turned and left him at the gate.

Dearmead held his throbbing ear and looked around the clearing to make sure nobody had seen the exchange.

Someone had.

A boy sat on a mossy boulder, face buried in a book, shoulders tensed and ears burning red. Dearmead took a deep breath and marched over to him.

"You got something to say?"

The boy raised his head and Dearmead realized he knew him.

Eaon Nemuse.

He had been one of four witchlings deemed too low in magic to be of use to the clan yesterday and would thus grow up to be a laborer or a traveler. Dearmead's fists clenched, worried his ma was still watching. That maybe she was testing him by humiliating him in front of one of his peers.

"Do it," Eaon said, looking down at Dearmead's fists.

"What?"

"You can hit me if you want. If it will make her leave you alone. I don't mind."

Dearmead blinked, too confused to reply. He'd spent his life trying to avoid getting hit, by his ma or da, by one of his older siblings or cousins. Everybody was always hitting each other in his house. They were fighters; it was what they did. And he hated it.

"Are you stupid?" Dearmead asked.

Eaon shrugged. "Depends who you ask. Are you going to hit me or not? Class is about to start."

That was when Dearmead noticed the slightly yellowed patch on Eaon's cheek.

The Nemuses were a powerful family, though Calla said they

were also a shrinking family. Having a laborer born into the mix probably hadn't been well received. He couldn't imagine it. If he had gone home to his ma last night and told her he had no magic, Mother be damned, she would have killed him.

Pity squeezed his chest. It was the kind of thing Calla had been trying to squash from him, but Dearmead couldn't bring himself to make Eaon's day any worse than it probably was.

"Then hurry up." Dearmead raised his chin and walked away.

<hr>

Things had changed since yesterday. Now that everybody had their test results, a clear division had been set between the students depending on the different magic they each possessed. Sitting on the floor of their classroom, huddled together toward the front of the room, were those with considerable blessings. The ones who had been showing signs for years already as well as the handful of dual-blessed witches: one Sanni- and Terra-blessed male, and two Terra- and Jem-blessed females. The rest of them, with the expected amount of magic displayed at their age, by far the largest group, were spread out and chattering loudly about the options they'd been given and what track they wanted to take in their secondary studies. Lastly, at the back of the room, the low-blessed. Those who would train to be laborers. Nobody spoke to them. Even between them, there were those from families with a long line of being low-blessed, and then there was Eaon. An outlier.

"Alright everyone, settle down," Teacher Teagan called as she sat at the front of the class, crossing her legs beneath her. "I know we're all very excited about the test results yesterday, but we still have a month left of elementary learning before you go to your separate secondary schools. So let's finish the year with some focus, okay?"

"Yes, Teacher Teagan," they all sang as one.

An elbow nudged Dearmead, and he turned to glance at one of his distantly related cousins sitting beside him.

"How come Unt Calla got stuck into you last night?"

"Shh."

"Is it because you got bad test results?"

"Yannis, shut up."

"Should you be sitting at the back of the room?"

Dearmead ignored him, but his ear started throbbing as if reminding him of why he really had gotten into trouble in the first place. Narrowing his eyes, he turned to his cousin. There was a gleam in his eyes that Dearmead was unsure about; was it because Yannis enjoyed teasing him, or was it because he knew the reason his ma had been angry with him? Was this a test?

Regardless, if Calla heard about this somehow, Dearmead couldn't deal with her being mad at him again. He shoved Yannis. His cousin grinned gleefully and shoved back.

"Weak."

"I'll show you weak," Dearmead hissed, balling his fists and pouncing.

The others around them scurried away as the two Bayfields landed hits on each other.

"Yannis! Yannis! Yannis!"

"Dearmead! Dearmead! Dearmead!"

Their teacher didn't bother to stop them, leaning against the wall of the hut and shaking her head. There was usually at least one fight between Bayfields at some point in the day.

Dearmead managed to pin down his cousin, knee digging into his stomach until Yannis tapped out. Equal shouts of disappointment and congratulations met him, but it rolled off his shoulders, meaningless. Everybody in his family was always teasing him for being soft, but he couldn't help that the fighting didn't heat his blood the way it did theirs. Didn't satisfy some innate calling in his soul.

As everyone settled down, Dearmead caught sight of Eaon once more. He wasn't watching. Squirreled away from everyone else, the Nemuse witch still had his head buried in his book.

Teagan raised her palms until silence once again descended.

"Alright, if we're ready to start," Teagan announced. "Group assignment."

A mixture of whoops and groans.

"Pair up, and your task for the day is to track and capture either a wattle bird or a field mouse. Before everyone crowds those on scout track, it's not about success today; it's about familiarizing yourselves with the animals that occupy our lands. Whether you become scouts or guardians, keepers or healers, bakers or tanners or gardeners, it is important to know as much as we can about Mother's creations and how they interact with the world. There is a lot to be learned. Tomorrow we will be writing reports about the process and what you discovered, and how this information may be useful to you in your future roles. I have already alerted the border guardians to what activity you are supposed to be doing, so don't think about slacking off."

Despite Teagan's instructions, the witchlings who'd bragged about their scout track results were immediately bombarded with pitches as to why they would make a good partner. Dearmead hadn't said anything about his test results, but a number of people came toward him knowing he'd done well in other tracking tasks over the years.

The only ones not bothering were the labor track witchlings. Nobody wanted to work with them, so they stuck together, discussing how they would go about finding a field mouse.

Except Eaon. Again, even among the laborers he was excluded, left to bury his nose deeper in the book he was reading.

"Hey, Dearmead!" someone called as they reached for him.

"Sorry, I already have a partner," he said, backing away.

It was probably a stupid idea, but he went and sat beside Eaon.

"Want to hunt down a wattle bird with me?"

Eaon's eyes stopped scanning the pages of his book, a shallow frown pulling down his brow. He looked to the group of witchlings nearby who seemed offended Dearmead had shrugged them off.

"Me?"

"You read a lot, so you probably already know a lot about them. I could use the help on the report tomorrow."

It was the truth. He might be good at scouting but he was rubbish at writing. Nobody else seemed to be thinking about the reports Teagan said they'd be doing tomorrow, but Dearmead was already dreading it. If there was one thing Calla hated more than Dearmead's spinelessness, it was his poor grades.

Eaon nodded, as if the match made sense to him too. "Alright. Your funeral."

"What do you mean?"

Eaon gave him a tired look, but when Dearmead still didn't understand what he meant, Eaon stood and put his book in his satchel.

"Let's just get this done."

---

Eaon was not quiet as they walked through the forest bordering Wyldeden, his footsteps breaking dry leaves and knocking stones, startling every mouse and bird within range. It wasn't

Eaon's fault, Dearmead reminded himself as he tried not to glare. It was magic that softened Dearmead's steps on the earth, magic that had stones and twigs rolling out of the way of his bare feet as he stalked through the bushes. That Eaon didn't even have enough magic for that . . . it wasn't his fault. Despite what everyone else seemed to think.

Distantly, the distinctive call of a wattle bird echoed through the towering shrubbery. Dearmead raised a hand, signaling for Eaon to stop walking.

As Dearmead listened for a second call, trying to pinpoint the direction, Eaon looked around wide-eyed. Finally, pointing east, Dearmead crept forward and Eaon did his best to follow.

When they reached the area he was sure the bird was, Dearmead leaped into a nearby tree, clambering up the branches as quietly as he had stalked the forest floor, eyes peeled for the flash of red or yellow among the unending landscape of browns and greens that would give the bird away. Eaon stayed on the ground, crouching with his paper and charcoal nib, watching Dearmead's technique as he tiptoed along the branch of the oak.

Everything heightened. Every scratch of the bark against his calloused feet told him how he needed to shift his balance, every rustling leaf as a soft breeze blew through the canopy whispered of the other wildlife holding still nearby as they sensed him creeping through their space. None of them twittered a warning to the wattle, none flew off, as if he wasn't a concern to them. As if he was one of them. And then he was on the same branch as the wattlebird, a yellow streak against the moss and foliage. It stilled, its beady black eyes locking onto Dearmead's frozen form, balancing on the toes of one foot, clutching the branch above in one hand, not daring to place the other down yet.

He'd seen drawings of panthers in encyclopedias, and he imagined himself as he must look to the bird, stalking among the shadows like a chunky baby wildcat. But he could not afford to be a predator if he wanted to catch a bird. Softening his stance with the speed of a sloth, he shifted his weight until he hung from the branch by his hands. The bird danced, fluffing its wings before returning its attention to the twig it was trying to peck free.

Glancing down, Eaon hadn't moved, still watching with his big amber eyes, the charcoal poised over his page.

A branch snapped somewhere nearby and Dearmead cussed, looking back to where the bird had turned in the direction of the sound, still as stone.

"Hey, is that you, Eaon?" someone called through the forest.

Eaon rose as another group came through the trees, not even trying to hunt. And while it was annoyance at the interruption that puckered Dearmead's brow, so close to touching the bird and completing the assignment, it was fear that somehow widened Eaon's eyes even further as he faced his cousin.

He took a step back just as the other Nemuse witch flung a rock, too slow to get out of the way. It glanced across his forehead, leaving a gash of dark mulberry red.

The wattlebird chittered, then took off.

"Let's go!" Dearmead called, hauling himself up into the branches and racing after it.

Below, Eaon kept pace.

Hollering laughter broke out as the other witches gave chase, flinging more rocks with about as much aim as a drunk with one eye.

"This way!" Dearmead called down, picking up speed before leaping freely from the oak to a nearby birch, the two branches a little farther apart than he would normally risk.

"Inna, wait! That's a Bayfield up there," the other witch called.

The chasing footsteps fell back, but Dearmead didn't slow down and Eaon hadn't even seemed to notice that they were no longer being pursued, fleeing like a hare through the shrubbery.

Dearmead heard the water long before they reached the edge of the forest, a rocky meadow on the border of the settlement coming into view. A river meandered lazily through it, stemming from a pool where a waterfall from the upper ledge of Wyldeden cascaded down in a deafening torrent. The wattle bird had fled the forest, flapping madly up the cliff face.

"Sorry," Eaon called, breathing hard as he watched it escape.

Dearmead let his momentum carry him from the tree, tucking and rolling as he landed in the meadow to stand by the river's edge.

"Not your fault."

Dearmead watched as Eaon crouched by the river to wash the blood from his face, keeping an eye on the tree line in case they were still being followed. Head injuries bled a lot, but Eaon would be alright. He just needed to learn to fight back.

They sat for a moment while Eaon pressed a hand to the wound, waiting for it to stop bleeding.

"You a good climber?" Dearmead asked as he turned back toward the cliff.

Eaon raised his eyebrow. "We'll just find another bird."

"No." Dearmead shook his head, heart racing so fast in his chest his body was half convinced he was still running. "I want that one."

"You'll never find it."

"Will too. I have its scent."

"Birds have scents?" Eaon asked skeptically.

Dearmead grinned. "To me they do. Teagan said I have one of the best senses of smell in the class. Bordering on animal, apparently, and likely a gift from one of the Spirits. I would be an awesome scout if I didn't have to be a guardian."

He realized too late that it was probably rude to be bragging to Eaon. There was a flash of pain and envy across his face before the frown came back. "Why do you have to be a guardian if you could be a scout?"

"My ma." He said it with a shrug and turned back to the cliff face, figuring out the best path up. He didn't want to talk about Calla. "I think we can do it if you strap your bag on your back."

Eaon was quiet for a moment, and Dearmead hoped he couldn't see the heat creeping up his neck. Eaon had seen Calla that morning, dragging Dearmead by his ear, telling him how weak he was. It was embarrassing.

"Okay then," Eaon said, adjusting the straps on his satchel until they twisted around his shoulders securely.

Dearmead led the way, taking the easiest path up the cliff where large flats jutted out like a natural, albeit convenient, staircase. He was so focused on finding the next handhold that he had no idea what Eaon was talking about when he called from behind, "Hey, what's that?"

Dearmead looked back to where Eaon was peering behind the sheet of water sliding over the rocks. A few feet away, there was a shadow too dark to be from a normal outcropping.

"Don't know." Dearmead shrugged. He took the next step up, grabbing a fistful of rock to keep steady, but Eaon didn't follow him. With a little jump to a narrow ledge, he crept his way toward the waterfall.

"I think there's something there."

"Eaon, come on," he called, heart still set on the wattle bird.

But Eaon ignored him, and before Dearmead could stop him, he took another short leap into the waterfall.

Holding a gasp, Dearmead waited for a scream. For Eaon to plummet back into the pool below. Waited, and waited.

"Whoa." Eaon's voice echoed from behind the waterfall. "You have to see this."

They were going to fail the assignment. His ma was going to belt him. But the wonder in Eaon's voice was too enticing to ignore, so he followed the path he had taken until he leaped through the thunderous water.

Not a ledge, but a cave. Sort of. More like a deep hollow, as if there had once been an enormous boulder that had fallen off when the cliffside eroded and left its crater behind.

The waterfall was loud and the gravelly ground was damp and cold, but it would make a hell of a hiding place.

"Cool." Dearmead smiled, and Eaon matched it.

CHAPTER 3
# THE CAVE

After a few minutes to explore the shallow cave, Dearmead convinced Eaon to come along and finish the assignment. It took most of the day to track down the exact bird Dearmead had set his sights on, but he was determined not to give up on it, and eventually his patience was rewarded. He held the wattle bird carefully in his cupped hands, letting Eaon take notes on how long it took the creature to settle.

"I can't believe you actually caught it," Eaon said quietly as Dearmead opened his palms. The wattle bird didn't fly away immediately, looking between the males curiously. From his satchel, Eaon pulled a small handful of seed and offered them to it, blinking in surprise as it hopped from Dearmead's palm to Eaon's, pecking lightly.

Beaming with pride, Dearmead took Eaon's notes and had a look at what he had recorded. Rough sketches of how Dearmead had poised in the tree, of the bird itself, the way Dearmead's hands had curled around it. Strings of words scrawled over the paper that Dearmead couldn't decipher.

"It's messy," Eaon said as he watched him. "When I write the actual report it won't be that bad."

"Better than mine," Dearmead said with a chuckle.

The bird finished the seed, took one last look between the two of them, then took off into the trees. They had chased it half way around Wyldeden, and as the sun began to head down toward the horizon, Eaon packed his notes away and started walking back in the direction of his house.

"What was it like?" Eaon asked.

Dearmead frowned as he followed. "What do you mean?"

"Tracking the bird. What does the magic feel like? What does it do? How does it help?"

Blinking a few times, Dearmead considered the questions. He had never tried to explain it before, and wasn't sure he knew how to put it in words.

"I just . . . need to know. For the report," Eaon explained, neck reddening at the lingering silence.

"Of course, I just . . . I'm not sure how to explain."

They walked along in silence for a while longer, stopping at a stream to drink. They hadn't stopped for lunch, Dearmead realized as his stomach started growling. Looking around, there was a communal apple orchard nearby.

"Hungry?" Dearmead asked, wandering over.

"Yeah." Eaon hurried after him.

The guardian patrolling the orchard, watching over the gardeners at work within, was one of Dearmead's distantly related unts, and she smiled as he approached.

"Finished school for the day?" she asked.

"Yeah, finally, but we missed lunch," Dearmead explained. "Thought we'd just grab something."

"Sure," she waved him through, then looked down at Eaon. "You're a Nemuse, right?"

Eaon nodded, eyeing the guardian's spear strapped diagonally across her back, the sharp stone tip poking over her shoulder.

"Ren?" she guessed.

"Eaon," he corrected.

She knew the name, her lips pursing. "Then I'm afraid you'll have to go home."

Both Dearmead and Eaon stared up at her, confused.

"Why?" Dearmead asked.

"We heard about his test results. Everybody has. Since he won't be contributing in any significant way, it's his family's responsibility to feed him now, not the clan's."

Color bloomed across Eaon's face as he took a step back. "Oh. Okay."

Dearmead's mouth fell open as he stared at his unt. He knew the laborers his family had hired relied on the Bayfields to keep them fed, clothed and housed in return for their service, but they were fully grown. Eaon was twelve, just like him. He wouldn't be a laborer for another thirteen years.

"That's not fair."

"Take what you need and go home, Dearmead."

He looked back to Eaon and muttered, "Go back to the stream. I'll be there in a minute."

Eaon nodded, eyes on his feet as he turned and walked away.

Quickly, Dearmead scaled the nearest tree and picked four apples, the brightest red and utterly flawless. Shoving two in his pockets, he jumped back down and took a bite from the one still in his hand, nodding to his unt.

"Both for you?" she asked with a warning in her tone.

"Yep."

"Go straight home, Dearmead."

"I heard you the first time."

He ran then, before his unt could scold him.

---

Back at the stream, Eaon sat and stared at the trickling water. Dearmead sat beside him and emptied his pockets, passing him both apples.

"Will you get in trouble?" Eaon asked, rubbing the fruit against his pants.

Dearmead shrugged and took a large, noisy bite, slurping the juice before it could trail down his chin.

Eaon seemed to grow even quieter. "Thanks."

"Thanks for doing the report," Dearmead countered. "Let me think about the magic stuff. Maybe after dinner we could meet back at that cave to talk about it?"

"We could just do that at school tomorrow," Eaon said before taking his own bite.

That was true. But the less time he had to spend at home, the less opportunity Calla had to come and interrogate him about his grades and whatever else she felt like getting on his back about.

"But," Eaon continued, looking at his apple. "It might be a good idea to stash some stuff in the cave. Just in case."

That was something Dearmead hadn't considered. He thought of the one non-school related book he had hidden in his room and the trouble he would be in if Calla caught him with it. Having a secret hiding place away from the estate would come in handy.

"So, the cave tonight?" Dearmead repeated, pleased when Eaon nodded.

Hiding in an alcove near the dining hall in the guardians' wing of the Bayfield estate, Dearmead waited until everyone else had filed in before taking a seat at the bench farthest away from his ma's place at the head of the room. Ignoring curious glances from the others, he ate as fast as he could before ducking back out.

From his bedroom—a small space with a down-stuffed mattress on a bed frame made of twisted willow—he pushed back the wooden shutters over the window and peeked outside. Not all houses in Wyldeden had shutters, but guardians sometimes worked nights and the coverings kept the sun out so they could sleep during the day.

The guardians patrolling outside the estate watched over the crops. Until now, Dearmead had never wondered why. They just did. But now he wondered if there were witches in Wyldeden, laborers with families who couldn't or wouldn't support them, who were hungry enough to try and steal food in the middle of the night.

Grabbing his book from under his pillow, Dearmead jumped out the window and snuck around the guardians on duty. The pathways along the valleys were lit with light-filled gemstones, courtesy of the Jem-blessed in Wyldeden. Small ones bordered the paths while larger ones were stuck in the ground like knee-high trees of rose quartz and topaz. Even without them, the Nemuse residence was renowned enough that he didn't need to see to find it.

The manor was reasonably close to the Bayfield estate, and the single guardian the family had hired to watch their crops was busy talking with someone in the gardens, so Dearmead had no trouble sneaking past. There was no sign of Eaon outside, so he skulked around the buildings, peering through windows until he found him in a small kitchenette with candles burning on the counter, sitting at a round table with his da and finishing a bowl of stew.

Ever so lightly, Dearmead tapped on the glass window. Both Eaon and his da turned at the sound, and Dearmead swore, ducking down. He didn't know Kailevi well, his gut churning at the idea that the male might tell Calla about this.

A moment later, the side door opened and Eaon stuck his head out. "I thought I was meeting you there."

"Your place was on the way," Dearmead shrugged. "Is your da going to let you go?"

"Yeah." He grinned, then turned back inside to tell Kailevi, "I'll be back before midnight, okay?"

"Have fun." Kailevi chuckled.

The relief was almost overwhelming. That wasn't the sound of someone who wouldn't like them sneaking around the settlement at night. He wouldn't get Dearmead in trouble.

With his satchel over his shoulder again, Eaon closed the door and the two of them aimed for the bordering forest.

---

Dearmead was rather embarrassed when they reached the cave and realized Eaon had the forethought to bring candles and matches, lighting one and leaving it as far from the wall of moving water as possible. Dripping wet, Dearmead took his book from under his arm and shook it dry. If he'd had any brains at all, he would have brought a satchel too.

"Lucky it's never cold here," Eaon chuckled, wringing out his shirt.

Dearmead frowned. "What do you mean?"

"Da says that when he's out traveling in the southern winter, getting wet is the best way to get hypothermia and die."

His mouth fell open. They had learned about the seasons in school, since some of them would inevitably end up outside the Boab at some point in their lives, but words like "cold" and "wind" and "snow" were still only abstract concepts to him. "What's hypothermia?"

"It's when your body gets so cold that your blood and skin freezes."

"And you can die from that?"

Eaon nodded, pulling a sack from his satchel and tucking it in the corner. "Want to put your book under this, so the water doesn't wreck it?"

Joining Eaon in the farthest corner, Dearmead stuffed his worn copy of *The Bee Keeper* under the sack. From the feel of it, Eaon had brought some non-perishable food to stash away.

"That's a good book," Eaon noted, tilting his head to read the title.

"You've read it?"

"Ages ago," Eaon nodded. "Why did you bring it here?"

"My ma doesn't like me reading."

Eaon frowned, genuinely perplexed. "Why?"

"Waste of time. But I like it."

He didn't mention that this was the only book he had ever read. Didn't mention that the only other one he'd ever managed to get his hands on had been taken and burned in the fire before he'd managed to read it.

"Me too. Did you figure out the magic stuff?"

They sat against the wall, the candle between them, and stared at the water thundering past. Patiently, Eaon waited as Dearmead struggled to explain what it felt like when his magic helped him hunt. Sometimes the probing questions Eaon asked sparked a train of thought, but most of the time they just left Dearmead stuttering for words.

Not once did Eaon make fun of him for struggling to speak. Not once did he sigh with impatience and give up waiting for Dearmead to figure out what he was trying to say. Eaon was nice in a way that most witches Dearmead had ever spent time with were not. In a way that made Dearmead hope that after tomorrow, when the assignment was over, they could be friends.

For the entire month left of their elementary schooling, Eaon and Dearmead met in the cave after dinner with their families. They were partners for every assignment, Dearmead doing the magic work and Eaon doing the academic stuff, trading notes and explaining the details to each other after hours. And when school was finally over and there were no more assignments to do, they sat quietly in the cave to read together. Eaon had a new book almost every day, going through twenty before Dearmead finished reading *The Bee Keeper* again, but he never mentioned it. Never teased Dearmead for how slow he was.

He finished the book and put it away again, watching Eaon read, entirely lost to the outside world. He held the pages so lightly, his fingers unconsciously stroking the edges of the parchment while they waited to turn it. Dearmead didn't want to interrupt him, even though he was curious as to what Eaon was reading. The title was a mash of letters he couldn't put together. But as he watched Eaon's hands, he noticed the faded bruises across his knuckles.

"Did you get in a fight?" he blurted out before he could stop himself. He had never seen Eaon fight, and it was such a strange thing to imagine, he had to find out if it was true.

"What?" Eaon frowned, putting the book down.

"Did you get in a fight?" Dearmead repeated, pointing to Eaon's hand.

"No?" He looked at his own knuckles, surprised to see the discoloring. "Oh."

Dearmead waited, but Eaon only pulled the book up to his face again. Slowly, other possibilities dawned on him. And he knew he should mind his own business, Mother knew Dearmead had his own family issues to deal with, and if anyone understood the need to avoid talking about them, he did, but it was different. When Dearmead was in trouble it was because of things he had done wrong, but if he was right about why Eaon's hand was bruised, then he was getting in trouble for things that were not his fault, and that wasn't fair.

"Want me to teach you how to fight back?" Dearmead offered.

Eaon's fingers stilled on the page, his eyes rising over the top of the book.

"What?"

"Want me to—"

"No, I heard you."

Closing his mouth, Dearmead frowned. Eaon pulled the book closer to his face until he couldn't possibly be reading it, resting his brow on the pages. Eventually, he asked quietly, "You . . . fight back?"

And so Dearmead told Eaon about how when a fight broke out with his brothers or sisters or cousins at home, he was expected to hit back. He was praised if he won and punished if he didn't, yet punished worse if he did not fight back at all. Even when his ma or da punished him, they wanted him to fight back. Though there would never be any winning against them.

Eaon was beyond perplexed. Turned out his own family was very different.

The Nemuse family might be shrinking, but there were still enough of them that Eaon could not walk through the halls of his house without at least one of them spitting at him, telling him how much they hated him for bringing shame to their family, or outright beating him. His parents argued every day with their Head of House about the way Eaon was being treated, but the Head was not inclined to care. Unlike Dearmead, fighting back would only make it worse.

All this, and he hadn't even started labor training yet.

Dearmead shook his head, horrified. "I didn't think anyone's family was as awful as mine."

The way Eaon's eyes widened made Dearmead grimace.

"I didn't mean—"

"No," Eaon interrupted. "They are awful. I just . . . the clan thinks my family are miracle workers. I didn't expect anyone else to admit that they're kind of shitty."

Dearmead nodded. That, he understood. "Nobody looks twice when Bayfields start fighting. And everyone else in my family is totally fine with things the way they are. They like it. They think it makes us stronger. Tougher. But I think they've all just taken so many blows to the head they don't have any brain cells left."

Eaon snorted, covering his mouth to stifle a laugh. Dearmead didn't hold back, grinning widely.

"Well, at least we have this place," Eaon said once he'd gotten a hold of himself.

"And each other," Dearmead insisted. "Because we're friends, right?"

Eaon stared at him for a long moment before nodding. "Yeah. That would be good. Friends."

# All Our Sharp Edges

# CHAPTER 4
# MARKING

Eaon had never been so tired.

In four years of secondary schooling on the labor track, not a single day had gone by that Eaon was not physically and emotionally exhausted. In the mornings, he had classes with the rest of his year level, learning history and community. He wasn't sure which he hated more: sitting in the back of the classroom listening to the raging superiority complexes of the witches and teachers around him, or his afternoons in laborer training.

Lunchtime was when everyone went to their respective specialty grounds, the guardians to their training rings, the gardeners to the fields to work with their mentors, etcetera etcetera. For Eaon, it meant going to the labor camps where he learned all the essential skills one needed to be of service to others, which at this point mostly involved learning how to bow correctly, how to address those with authority, and how to not get in people's way. How to be appropriately grateful for being cared for, despite having nothing of worth to offer. Hours of lectures, making sure he and the others understood their place before being sent to their mentors to learn how to clean and cook and grovel.

He wasn't at all bitter about it.

But he supposed it could be worse. At least he was able to go home to be mentored.

Though his da spent eighty percent of his time doing traveling work, either from within the Boab or outside of it, the twenty percent between expeditions he was made to labor too, and Eaon was able to work with him. When Kailevi was away, the few laborers the Nemuse family were still able to employ took over.

He was lucky he wasn't one of the laborers who came from a long line of low-blessed witches, or those whose families were not large enough to have a laborer quota applied to them. Lucky he didn't have to stay at the camps.

Run by teachers who'd drawn the short straw, the worse-off laborers-in-training stayed behind to learn from the tertiary students, or from those who had graduated into full-time laborers but did not have an employer at all. They offered their services back to the camps in exchange for shelter and whatever scraps of food the teachers could spare for them.

It was a fate his new Head of House often threatened Eaon with whenever he couldn't swallow his bitterness completely. They didn't have to keep him in their home. They didn't have to feed him and clothe him and let him stay with his parents and sister. Anytime they chose, they could ship him off to the camps to live where he could fight over scraps and beg for a chance to work for someone.

If Dearmead ever heard about it he would promise him a place in the Bayfield residence, but Eaon wasn't sure the shredded remains of his pride could handle that. Or that he could handle Calla.

"No, no, no," his mentor Maerie moaned as she ran to where Eaon squatted by the stream that ran alongside the Nemuse manor, washing blood from the skirts of one of his older cousins. She had recently undertaken the fertility ritual so she could breed, and her first bleeding had been brutal. "Eaon, what have you done?"

Blinking back the haze in his eyes, he looked at the cloth in his hands. The cloth he had been scrubbing at for Mother knew how long. The fabric had pilled and become threadbare from over-washing.

"Fuck."

"Watch your mouth," she hissed, snatching the skirt from him. "I'll fix it."

But as she stalked away, Eaon heard the words she muttered under her breath.

"Never seen a more useless laborer."

It was the lowest work, and he was still terrible at it.

"I'm sorry," he called out, getting to his feet to fetch something else to clean. One of the tertiary laborers working with Maerie was picking through the basket, eyeing him as he came near.

"Why don't you go see if Tonia needs help in the kitchen before Maerie kills you," Meenis said.

Eaon wanted to smack that smirk right off his face, the way Dearmead always told him he should, but he'd never get away with it. Biting his tongue until he tasted blood, fighting the urge to cry from the tired ache in his knees as he wiped his wet hands on his trousers, he went to find Tonia in the main kitchen.

It was easily four times the size of the little kitchenette he and his da ate alone in every day, and with Nemuse numbers dwindling, there was really only the four of them left to work.

"No. No, no, no," Tonia said as Eaon eased open the door. "Absolutely not."

"Maerie and Meenis said—"

"No, I'd rather do all this by myself."

Eaon sighed, resting his forehead against the doorway. "I promise I won't burn anything this time."

"You say that, but I don't believe you. Go make yourself useful down at the chicken coop or something."

"I already did the chickens."

"The goat then."

"I did the goat."

"Then go and take the manure to the gardeners for composting." Tonia shooed him away with a wooden spoon covered in sauce.

"I need to learn this," Eaon said, looking around the kitchen. "You guys are supposed to be my mentors—"

"And as your mentor, I'm telling you to go and bother someone else! I'm not getting in trouble again because you're a useless cook!" she shouted.

Grinding his teeth, Eaon slammed the door and stormed down the hall.

They always left the manure to him, carrying it across the valleys in buckets to where the gardeners made compost for the communal crops. He hadn't vomited from the smell in years, but he still lost his appetite for the rest of the day afterward. All the others jobs were on rotation, everyone taking a turn, but that job was just for him. Because unlike Maerie and Meenis and Tonia, he was a Nemuse. He was one of *them*. And any opportunity to remind him that he would never belong anywhere, they took it.

Standing in the manor's primary doorway, the animal pens

goading him, Eaon closed his eyes and tried to take a steadying breath. Which was a mistake. Opening them again felt like splitting wood.

There were still a few hours left in the day, and it only took him one to get to the composter's.

He just needed a rest. Just a few minutes to close his eyes.

Using the wall to keep himself steady, Eaon made his way to his room.

---

Being dragged out of bed by his ankle woke him two seconds before his head hit the floor.

His cousin, the one whose skirt he had ruined, seethed at him. "Maerie told me it was you who ruined my skirt, and then you have the audacity to take a nap? Lazy little shit!"

Eaon pulled his foot away, scowling as he sat up. "I'm not feeling well."

"Do I look like I care? You're the one who lost my favorite blouse, too, aren't you?"

Eaon frowned. He didn't know anything about a lost blouse. "No?"

"Liar," she hissed. "I'm going to tell the Head of House—"

"No! Wait! I . . . I didn't lose your blouse, but I . . . I'll make you a new one."

His cousin snorted, looking down at him with derision before heading to the door.

"Lina, don't." Eaon scrambled up from the floor and chased his cousin as she stormed down the hall. "I'm trying, okay? Give me a chance to find it."

"So you admit you lost it."

"No, I don't know anything about it, I swear on the Mother."

She turned around and slapped him. "Don't you dare lie on her name."

"I'm not!"

She hit him again, and his fists curled. Only the training he endured in the camps let him swallow down his anger, focusing on his shoes so she wouldn't see how badly he wanted to hit her back.

"Admit it, or I'll make you."

He didn't know what that meant, but by the vicious tone in her voice he guessed he didn't want to.

"I promise, I am not lying."

She shook her head. "Bow to me."

He couldn't help it, he glared at her with all his sour resentment.

"Bow to me right now, laborer," she snarled at him, "or I'll go right to the Head and he can deal with your disobedience and lying."

Shaking from his hatred, he made himself bow as low as he had been taught to. His cousin grabbed the back of his shirt and yanked it over his head, tangling him up in it until he couldn't see. He tried to pull away, to stand, but she pinched a nerve in the back of his neck that sent pain cascading into his forehead.

Fucking healers.

"Now," she said slowly, dragging something cold across his bare back in a pattern of lines. "Tell me the truth."

A spellmark, he realized, stomach clenching as magic swelled in the hall, splitting open his skull. It reached inside his head, down his throat, and dragged the words out.

"The sun in Nir is our planet's closest star and rises in the east, sets in the west. The version we have in Wyldeden—"

"No." She shoved him back, ripping his shirt with her long nails. "Tell me the truth about the blouse!"

But he had not finished fulfilling her first request, every truth he knew pouring out if his mouth as he knelt on the ground before her.

"—rises north and sets south. It is during the sunrise that you undertook the fertility ritual last week with your friends and now you're trying to conceive with the baker's son who lives across the valley, but everybody says he's not worthy of you and would produce weak offspring. Besides, he'll likely die of a heart attack before you get a chance."

"Shut up!" she hissed, stepping back so she had room to kick him in the face.

His head hit the wall and the added pain pushed him over the edge. Bile came burning up his throat, but he couldn't stop talking, even as he vomited all over himself.

"Salt water is not safe to drink," he choked, "as the sodium component dehydrates you faster than the water can satiate it. In the western territories, sea witches desalinate the water—"

He wanted to beg her to take the mark off his back, but he had lost control of his mouth. Eyes blurring with pain and panic, he watched his cousin spit at him before stalking down the hall.

It was getting dark.

A number of his unts and unks passed him by, carrying candles, ignoring him. He couldn't get up, couldn't move, the pain of the spellmark on his skin drawing a fresh wave of nausea every time he tried.

And he was still talking.

"Anfar was won during the Third war, but it is not ruled by the Anfar Forest Clan. Despite a number of covens and rogues staking claims on parts of the land, it is technically free for any Terra witch to live on if they are able."

Another of his cousins chuckled as they walked past him, their candle light disappearing into the dark hall.

*Please*, he screamed silently to nobody. *Please make it stop.*

"There are seven elemental spirits with realms that lay parallel to Mother's, plus her Lover's, which are the void and the after realm. Then there is also Morvia's realm, which is unknown to all who are not blessed by her. Mother and the Lover, life and death, create Balance, and so they are considered the High Spirits, whereas the seven elementals are responsible for the different aspects of Mother's realm. Nature, the sea, fire, the sky, silver, crystal, and bodies."

It was at least another hour before someone else came down the hall.

Someone he was beyond glad to see.

"Oh, Eaon." His da sighed, crouching beside him.

Tears welled as Eaon said, "The deadliest snake in the world is the adder, which is identifiable—"

"Let's get you to your ma," Kailevi said, scooping Eaon off the floor.

A wave of nausea rolled through him, but there was nothing left to throw up. Still, his head spun with dizziness, and the heaving gave him a second's break from talking.

---

Kailevi put Eaon down on his bed and smoothed back his hair before calling for Ellissa. Eaon's voice was cracking, half his words only a rasp now.

"The high priestess of Wyldeden has the strongest Terra

blessing the clan has ever seen, hence why she is trusted above all others to rule."

Ellissa's footsteps did not make sound, but his door creaked as she entered, Eavha trotting behind her. His sister's eyes widened as she took in Eaon's shaking, pain ridden body, the useless information spewing out of his mouth garbled with exhaustion.

"Someone marked him," Kailevi said, rolling Eaon onto his side to pull away his ruined shirt.

"I'll get the vinegar and sea salt to scrub it off," Ellissa said, hurrying back out to the hall.

"We're going to get it off you and it will stop, okay?" Kailevi promised, drawing a sob of relief out of Eaon.

Eavha came to his bedside and lay one of her small hands on his elbow.

Magic swelled, and Eaon flinched. But the magic didn't hurt this time. As it washed over him, the splitting pain inside his skull dulled. The nausea settled.

His voice cleared as he said, "There are forty-two languages spoken in Nir, with Nirnish being the most common. The fae and early witches thought humans lacked the intelligence to learn other languages, so they renamed the human tongue and deemed it the national language in an effort to be inclusive."

Ignoring Eaon's continued rambling, Kailevi looked down at Eavha. "Petal . . ."

She was due to take her tests in a few weeks and she had been showing signs of being a strong healer for a while, but she had not even spoken. Had not used a mark or enchantment to channel it.

She left her hand on Eaon, the air rippling with magic until Ellissa came back. His ma gasped loudly and grinned.

"Oh, my sweetheart." Sitting beside her on Eaon's bed, dampening a salt block with vinegar to scrub at whatever his cousin had used to draw the mark on his back, Ellissa's attention was on Eavha. "You sweet girl. How are you doing that, honey?"

"I just didn't want him to be in pain, and it happened," she answered.

Eaon closed his eyes. The pain had eased, but a new one that had nothing to do with what his cousin had done bloomed in his chest.

He knew what it was, and he hated it.

Jealousy.

"I want to die," the words fell out of him just a moment before the spellmark was finally broken enough to stop affecting him. "I hate my life and I want the Lover to take me next."

The room was silent, his ma's hands stilling on his back. The magic in the room faltered. Then there was sobbing, and Eaon had no idea who it was coming from.

---

The sun through the window woke him but he was too tired to open his eyes. Too exhausted to move his body. The sheets were tangled in a sweaty mess around his long and lanky legs, his hair plastered to his face.

The whispering in his room suggested his ma and da, who had not left all night, did not know he was awake yet.

"You heard what he said, Kai. We can't do nothing."

"I know."

"We have to tell them."

"Elly, it's not safe."

"You keep saying that, but keeping quiet isn't safe for him either."

"It's a different kind of unsafe. Besides, without proof, who would believe us?"

"You're proof."

"I can't, Elly."

"You have to. Or else we have to undo it."

"I can't do that either."

Ellissa sat down on Eaon's bed, unaware that he was listening. "And I can barely look at him after the way my family treats him. I can't stand it. So what are we going to do?"

Birds outside began to chirp and Eaon took a long, sullen breath. He would have to get up soon. There were chores to be done before school.

"Get to work, Elly. I'll figure this out. I promise."

"Look after him today."

"I won't leave his side. And I'll try to delay my next trip."

Ellissa stroked Eaon's hair before leaving. His eyes burned. He was too old to want so much to curl up in his ma's lap and let her sing him to sleep, but he doubted she would—even if he found the nerve to ask. She could barely stand to look at him, after all.

Finally, he opened his eyes. The sunlight made him want to vomit again as a deep ache throbbed in his head.

"Hey," Kailevi said from the chair he'd dragged into Eaon's room at some point during the night. "How are you feeling?"

Eaon just stared at him.

Grimacing, Kailevi plucked a vial from the dresser and came to sit beside him. "Your ma brewed this for you. It will help with the fatigue. And your mood."

Eaon didn't move.

"Come on. Sit up."

When Eaon still didn't respond, Kailevi put the vial back down.

"I know it's hard—"

"No you don't."

His voice scraped, throat tight and jaw aching.

Kailevi might have to labor when he was between traveling trips, but he was not of Nemuse blood. They didn't hate him the way they hated Eaon. Nobody had ever done to Kailevi what they did to him.

"Eaon, I need to know who marked you. It's against the law for anyone below an elder to mark another witch."

He knew that, but it didn't matter. His cousin would only find a way to make him pay for ratting and he couldn't be bothered dealing with it. So he ignored Kailevi's question, looking down to a crack in the floor instead.

After a while, Kailevi sighed.

"We'll do better. We're going to protect you better, I promise. But you have to tell me. And you have to get up, Eaon."

"I'm too tired." He hadn't meant for his voice to break, eyes filling once more. But he just couldn't do it. If he got up, then he had to work. Had to see his family. Had to go to school and sit beside all the people who didn't have to live his life. But if he stayed in bed, he didn't have to do any of it.

"The Head of House will not be happy with you if you don't get up," Kailevi warned, not as a threat, but as if he could read Eaon's mind and was reminding him why staying in bed for the rest of his life was not an option.

Closing his eyes again, Eaon couldn't stop the dampness rolling down his face.

"It's going to be alright," Kailevi said, squeezing his arm. "I'm right here. One step at a time, alright? Let's sit up."

Grip tightening on Eaon's arm, Kailevi helped him sit up in bed. His head spun, eyelids far too heavy.

"Alright. Now, drink."

Kailevi put the vial of tonic against Eaon's lips, and he parted them enough to drink it down.

"Well done. Let's give that a moment to do its work. Have some water."

A glass was placed to his mouth, and he drank that too.

One step at a time, Kailevi talked Eaon through getting out of bed. Through dressing and eating breakfast. Then he sent a whispering leaf to Eaon's teacher to excuse him for the day, making Eaon sag at the table in relief.

"You stick with me today, alright? You can do this. We just have to do what has to be done."

Eaon nodded. "Thanks, Da."

"I've got you, alright? I've got you."

## CHAPTER 5
# BOOKS

When the news came that another Nemuse witch had passed, Dearmead almost fainted from the panic. Eaon had been missing a lot of school lately, and nobody would tell him who it was that the Lover had taken. Not until he tracked down one of Eaon's cousins and pinned them to the wall.

"No, it's not Eaon!" he spat at Dearmead. "Oaf."

Dearmead shoved him away. "That wasn't hard, was it?"

"One of these days it will be him, though," the Nemuse witch sneered. "I pray for it. We all do."

Red clouded Dearmead's vision and he reached for the witch again, eager to make him eat his own teeth. Too quick, the witch dodged out of the way, tripping over himself to sprint off toward the communal gardens.

Later. He would get him later.

Unable to focus, the afternoon was grueling. The guardian training grounds had been flooded on purpose, their teachers watching them go through warm-ups in the mud. Throwing himself into the exercise was at least a way to work off the frustration and panic and generally foul mood he was in, but after that were drills that required more focus than he could muster. He was out of sync, forgetting the next stance he was supposed to move into, and the teachers prowling the lines noticed. Took notes.

Calla would be having words with him tonight, that was for sure.

Eventually, training was over and Dearmead took a long soak in the river to scrub himself clean before making his way to the cave. Eaon hadn't been for a while, but it was still a good place to hide away until he had no choice but to go home and face his ma.

There was a charm project he was behind on, so in the seclusion of the cave behind the waterfall, Dearmead worked on imbuing the twine between his fingers with magic.

Footsteps on the rocks outside made him pause.

"Eaon?" he called out hopefully.

Sure enough, the water broke for a moment as Eaon jumped through, shaking his mousy curls dry.

"Hey." He sounded tired. Looked it, too. Deep shadows under his eyes, cheekbones jutting out farther than the last time he'd seen him, he looked like he hadn't slept or eaten in days.

"You alright?"

"Yeah."

Sitting down, Eaon immediately grabbed a book and opened to where he'd left his bookmark. It was normal for them to sit in silence together, doing their own things, but something was off today.

"I heard you had another passing."

"Mmhm."

"Who was it?"

"Cousin."

"Isn't that, like, thirteen this year?"

"Yup."

"Does it worry you that your family is shrinking so quickly?"

"No." But there were tension lines around Eaon's eyes.

"You'd care if it was your ma or da, though, right?"

Eaon grimaced. "It would be an honor."

Dearmead rolled his eyes and scoffed. "Oh, don't give me that shit."

With a slow blink, Eaon raised his eyes from his book.

"I get it," Dearmead continued. "You have to say the right thing all the time. But I'm telling you right now, if it was my family being reaped the way yours is I would be scared shitless."

Crossing his legs, Eaon lowered his book. "Something on your mind, Dea?"

Dearmead opened his mouth, but nothing came out. Eaon waited patiently until he finally managed, "I thought it was you."

He expected laughter. Then he remembered that Eaon never laughed at him, so he waited for the reassurance. But it didn't come. Eaon's gaze dropped to his feet, the breath leaving him in a weary sigh.

"If the idea of my death worries you so much, maybe you should make other friends."

Dropping the twine, Dearmead's shoulders stiffened as he watched Eaon shrink in on himself. There was something wrong. He could sense it.

"Did something happen?"

Sniffing, Eaon raised his book once more. "I came here to relax, not for therapy."

Well, fine. If that was how he wanted to be, then fine. Picking up his twine, Dearmead went back to trying to charm it. As he rallied his magic and offered it to Terra, he began the incantation again.

"Could you not do that right fucking now?" Eaon snapped.

The magic died off, and Dearmead stared. But Eaon was not looking at him.

"What's your problem?"

"I have a headache."

Bullshit. But Dearmead put the twine aside and picked up a loose pebble, throwing it at the water and watching it disappear. Eaon wasn't the only one in a bad mood, but Dearmead wasn't biting his head off.

"Get a tonic for it then."

"I already took one."

He hated this. It was tempting to leave the cave, leave Eaon to his moping. But that was also the last thing he felt like doing. The irony of him wanting Eaon to just *talk* to him was laughable, considering Dearmead's own trouble doing so, and he didn't know what to do to draw Eaon out.

"Why do you read so much?" Dearmead snapped stupidly instead of throwing another rock through the waterfall.

"Why do you breathe so much?" Eaon muttered back, turning a page.

Dearmead rolled his eyes. "To live, obviously."

"Well there you have it."

"You don't need books to live."

"Says you." Eaon twirled his wrist. "I would have thrown myself into the Lover's void by now if I didn't have books."

Dearmead's heart skipped a beat, but at least Eaon was engaging now. "What could possibly be that great about it?"

"If you have to ask, then you're reading the wrong books."

As if he had been given the choice. The freedom. Dearmead

kept his mouth shut, but his gaze flickered over to his secret copy of *The Bee Keeper*. It was still the only book he had ever read that wasn't for school, and he hadn't touched it in years.

As Eaon realized what he'd said, he lowered his book again.

"This one is about a sea witch who falls in love with a mermaid, but because the mermaid is a beast she has to fight the urge to kill and eat the witch all the time, and there ends up being a war between the witch's coven and the mer folk," he explained.

"That . . . actually sounds pretty cool," Dearmead admitted. "Who writes these things anyway?"

"Witches in other clans that are allowed to do cool stuff like that," Eaon grumbled. "Da brought this one back from the river clan for me. I have the whole series. You can borrow them if you want."

Dearmead considered it. "I don't know. If its special to you I'd better not take it home. If ma found me with it—"

Eaon was immediately pissed. "So keep it here."

Again, Dearmead was tempted. "I don't know."

"Alright then, whatever."

And he was gone again, hiding in the yellowing pages of his merfolk fantasy. Dearmead tossed the rock in his hand. In the four years they had been coming here together, Eaon had never asked about why Dearmead only read the one book. At first he had thought Eaon assumed he was stupid. Then, the more he'd gotten to know him, he figured Eaon was just too polite to bring it up. Or perhaps he legitimately didn't care about Dearmead's reading habits. This was the first time he'd offered to lend him a book, but Dearmead had never asked before either.

He couldn't tell anyone else, but Eaon . . . Eaon was different.

"I'm not great at reading," he blurted out.

Eaon lowered his book.

"The words get all mixed up," he continued, squaring his shoulders. "I probably couldn't get through it."

Eaon blinked. Twice. "Okay. Well, we could read it together, if that would help."

After four years, Dearmead was still surprised when Eaon didn't laugh at him. Was still taken aback by his kindness.

"You're almost finished it." Dearmead shook his head, his face heating.

"Yeah, but I'm not ready for it to end yet. I don't mind starting again."

And without waiting for further arguments, Eaon turned the book back to the start and began to read aloud.

---

Enraptured by the story, Dearmead forgot about dinner. When Eaon's voice grew tired they realized it had gotten late and both of them would be in trouble. But Eaon promised to keep reading tomorrow, so Dearmead went home, playing the story out in his head again. It was a different kind of magic, he thought, to create a new world with only words.

A new world he wished he could escape to as he climbed through his bedroom window to find his ma waiting, arms crossed against the wall.

"What kind of time do you call this?" she asked.

"Lover take me, Ma, don't you have anything better to do than worry about what I do in my spare time?"

The attitude in his words didn't match the rabbit-footed thrumming of his heart, eyes scanning his room for a weapon.

"I have so many other things to worry about it's ridiculous, which is why having to divert time to finding out why you're slipping behind in classes again is annoying, to say the least."

"I'll catch up. I always do."

"After a little motivating."

Tensing, Dearmead waited for her to make the first move. Calla's eyes glittered as she watched him shift into a defensive posture.

"Where were you tonight, Dearmead?"

He wouldn't tell her. No matter how hard she kicked his ass tonight, the hours spent in the cave with Eaon, getting lost in a beautiful fantasy world together, was something he would not let her take from him.

It must have shown on his face, because Calla's crooked mouth turned up into a wicked smile.

"Outside. Ten minutes."

Dearmead sagged and ran his hands through his hair as she left. His black mane was getting long now. Past his shoulders. Some considered it a liability to have hair long enough to grab, to pull, but he liked it. Taking the piece of twine he had failed to enchant, he braided his hair and tied it up. Then he went out to meet Calla for one of her famous motivational lessons.

# CHAPTER 6
# FRENZY

It was that time of year again.

They weren't technically supposed to celebrate birthdays that weren't milestones, but Eaon had been so unwell of late that Kailevi was making his favorite aubergine lasagne for dinner to try and lift his spirits.

He should be studying for his history exams, but he had hidden the biography of an old traveler inside his homework instead, his nose buried in it as he waited at the little round table.

But he couldn't focus on it properly. Couldn't focus on anything.

In the adjacent dining room, the excitable chatter from the rest of the family spilled out. He knew what they were talking about; today had been Eavha's final test. She had received her role recommendations and, rather than come home afterward, she had gone straight to the healer's clinic to tell them she would soon be joining them.

Nobody was surprised.

But one look at Eaon's face and Kailevi had known that, no matter how pleased he was for his sister, the jealousy was eating him alive.

The door to their kitchen opened and Ellissa and Eavha came skipping in, hand in hand.

"Da!" she squealed when she saw Kailevi, running and leaping into his arms the moment he put the ladle down. "Look!"

She showed him the slip of parchment that had her grades on it while Ellissa turned to Eaon, who was trying to keep his face neutral.

"Congratulations, petal," Kailevi beamed, stroking back her wild hair. "I knew you would do amazing."

"Did you read the part that says I was the best in the entire grade?" Eavha said, waving her parchment around, bursting with pride. "The best the High Teacher had ever seen? She said I had potential to be a priestess one day!"

He should congratulate her. Should say something. Anything.

Putting his book down, he tried to quiet the ringing in his ears. Tried to settle the shaking in his hands, the twisting in his gut, the rawness of his throat.

"How was your day, Eaon?" his ma said softly, sitting across the table from him.

How was his day?

A dark, bitter laugh bubbled its way out as he stared at his ma, then at his sister, who had stopped bragging long enough to notice him.

"Perfect," he hissed, another painful bout of hysterics clawing its way out. "Just perfect."

"Hey," Kailevi said gently, abandoning the stove. "Let's go for a walk."

"No need." Eaon raised his hands, the laughter dying off. "I know. Shut up and worship my all-powerful little sister."

"Eaon."

"Because she's so fucking special, right? She's so fucking amazing! Yay for Eavha!"

"Eaon, enough," Ellissa warned as she tried to grab his hand, but he pulled it away, shoving his books off the table to scatter across the floor.

Eavha's eyes glistened with tears as she clutched her parchment to her chest.

He got off his chair and dropped to his knees. "Praise for Eavha! Priestess? Pah! High priestess! Goddess! Ruler of the entire fucking world!"

"Enough," Kailevi grabbed him by the back of his shirt and hauled him to his feet. "Let's go. Now."

"Don't fucking touch me!" Eaon spat, pulling away. "Wouldn't want you to catch my uselessness."

The pain in Kailevi's eyes only made Eaon laugh again. The door between their suite and the main dining room was opening, one of his cousins sticking their heads in to see what the commotion was about.

"Oh, they're waiting for you." Eaon looked down at Eavha and pointed to the door. "Go be with your people."

"I hate you," she whispered as she stormed toward their cousin, who waved a hand to hurry her.

"Join the club!" Eaon spat after her.

"Why do you have to make everything about you!" she screamed back.

Her words were a spear to the gut as she slammed the door between them.

"I understand this is difficult for you," Ellissa started, reaching for Eaon's arm again.

"Stop trying to touch me! Don't fucking touch me! You know nothing! You understand nothing!" he shouted at her, but his voice cracked.

He was the sour grape on the vine. He was the rotten apple on the tree. He could feel it, the disgust, the hatred, the bitterness that he existed at all. Eavha, his parents . . . their shame of him. Felt it crawling over his skin, wrapping its fingers around his throat. Worse still, he couldn't even keep his rottenness to himself. He had to spread it around.

Selfish. Useless and selfish.

Fists clenched, he hit himself in the side of the head. Then again. Again, again, again, until Kailevi was in his space, grabbing his wrists, wrestling them down.

"Stop. Stop," his da begged. Ellissa was crying at the table, her head in her hands.

"Let me go," he hissed, pulling back, throwing himself against the wall and taking Kailevi with him. Smashing his head against the stone, red spotted across his vision. So he did it again. He wanted to do it until his brain was soup. Until he couldn't think anymore. Until he couldn't be anything anymore.

Wrapping his arms around Eaon's body, Kailevi lifted him up and over his shoulder like a sack of grain.

"Put me down!"

But his da ignored him, taking him outside and away from the house.

He didn't care who saw him, he kicked and scratched and hit at Kailevi, hating him and hating himself. Hating everything. Hating everyone. But as if he was no more annoying than a blowfly, Kailevi kept walking all the way into the forest by their house before putting him down carefully. Keeping a hold of his wrists, Kailevi held Eaon close as he twisted and screamed and beat at his da as hard as he could. For minutes or hours, he didn't know, but as suddenly as the fit had come on it was over. His knees gave out and he dropped, exhausted and on the verge of vomiting.

Kailevi sat down, silent as he eased his grip on Eaon's wrists.

"It's not fair," his da finally said.

Eaon only sniffed, too tired to speak. Clarity was sneaking in, and holding its hand was shame. And fear. The scene he'd caused tonight would not have gone unnoticed, and the Head of House would make sure there were consequences.

And with that thought alone, a fresh swell of violence had him trying to smash his own head in again. As he thrashed and screamed at his da, he was vaguely aware that someone else had joined them. He was being pinned down, his head held still as a vial was put to his lips. Hoping it was poison, he drank greedily. And when it fogged his mind and made his body too heavy to move, he succumbed to it.

Groggy, Eaon woke in his own bed. For a moment, he didn't know why he was there. Couldn't remember what had happened. Then he tried to move and the bone-deep ache in his body brought the violence of the night right back.

"Shh," his ma said softly, sitting on the bed beside him. "I'm nearly done."

Her hands, covered in burnt herbs, hovered over his face as she slowly eased the throbbing pain in his head. Eaon looked around for his da, the dawn light graying his cluttered bedroom, piles of books in every corner with bits of leaves or flowers sticking out of them to keep his place. But there was no sign of Kailevi, and Eaon shuffled uncomfortably.

It was rare that Ellissa spent time with Eaon. Whether it was an intentional distance, he didn't know, but it was notable. All they ever did was exchange small talk or sit in silence while Ellissa healed his injuries, and even then, Kailevi or Eavha was usually around.

He wasn't even sure he remembered the last time his ma smiled at him.

"I'm sorry." The words were pitiful and he was embarrassed for even having said them.

"I'm sorry I had to sedate you, but you weren't calming down. I didn't want you to keep hurting yourself."

"Da . . ."

"He's fine."

"He hates me."

"No." Her voice turned sharp and hard. "No he does not. And before you even think it, neither do I. And no matter what she says, neither does Eavha. I explained things to her, and she just wants you to feel better."

Eaon lay still as his ma muttered a quiet prayer to finish healing him to the best of her ability. The assurance was difficult to believe.

"What did you tell her?"

Ellissa sighed, lowering her hands and smoothing back his hair. The touch was warm and gentle, not at all the harsh hand he knew he deserved.

"I've seen this kind of thing before at the clinic. Emotions that are too strong, that change too quickly. You get so down, Eaon. And you're so angry. And you have a right to be, but last night . . . You're not well. And it's okay, it's not your fault. I'm going to brew you a tonic that will help keep everything at a more . . . manageable level, okay?" She rested a hand over his sluggish heart, her voice lowering as she averted her eyes. "I know we ask a lot of you. To stay strong, to do what needs to be done until Eavha's old enough to leave the family too. It's not fair, and I'm sorry too, because I haven't been paying enough attention. I know how stress can affect a person. So I want you to know you can talk to me, okay? And your da is talking to Eavha about trying to be a bit more sensitive."

"She deserved to be happy," was all Eaon said. It was too much all at once. He hated that he was a burden on them, and this matter about his moods only added to his self-loathing, but . . . if a taking a daily tonic would make him more bearable to be around then that was what he would do.

"I wish you were happy, too," Ellissa said, putting her forhead against his and closing her eyes.

Eaon turned away. Happiness wasn't on the cards for him. Not as long as he was stuck with this family that hated him. In this clan that bemoaned his uselessness. In this Boab, that felt more and more like a cage.

Again, he stayed home from school. The tonic his ma had given him left him sluggish and scatterbrained, but the wildfire that had burned through his veins the night before, through his every thought and breath and heartbeat, had been smothered. He could barely rally the cohesiveness to read, let alone ruminate on last night.

"Too strong," Kailevi had noted, sending a whispering leaf to Ellissa. "Much too strong."

A messenger arrived around noon to deliver his progress report for school, but Kailevi simply tucked it into his pocket and continued to show Eaon how to find food in the wild.

"Just in case," he'd said as he took Eaon into the forest again, pointing out where edible mushrooms grew and how to tell the difference between them and the toxic ones.

Just in case their Head of House decided he wasn't worth feeding at some point, was what Kailevi didn't say. Eaon couldn't find the energy to care.

But later that night, long after both he and Eavha were supposed to have gone to bed, he knew they would look at his grades. He also knew he shouldn't listen, but he couldn't help himself as he snuck out to eavesdrop. Their voices were lowered, wine goblets clinking on the kitchen table as they talked over his school report by candlelight.

"Look at this," his da spat.

"I know."

Stomach curdling in shame, he closed his eyes.

"He's obviously got a skill for language. For history and reasoning. He would make a fantastic teacher. Aside from conducting magic classes, he wouldn't need any of his own. Someone else could run just that portion. Or he could be a keeper in one of the libraries. How many magical tasks could they possibly need in there? He could easily work there." Kailevi was getting worked up, as he always did when it came to anything to do with Eaon.

"Hush, Kai. You'll wake them."

"This is bullshit."

"I know it is. I know. But what can we do? The elders will not make an exception for him. If they did, they would have to make one for everyone. His best chance is for us to keep pushing for him to be allowed to travel," Ellissa insisted.

Eaon's heart was racing. Was it possible? Was any other track aside from the one he was on possible?

"There's no demand for more travelers," Kailevi argued. "They'll push him into laboring, I just know it. And look, Elly.

With grades this low in laboring disciplines, they'll leave him in the camps."

There was a moment of silence before Eaon realized his ma was crying. "I'll talk to the laborers here. Make sure they're helping him."

"You know they're not. They won't. I'm telling you, Elly, we have to make sure this doesn't happen. He cannot labor. And traveling with me . . . it's not ideal. And it'll take a miracle to pull off. I don't want to count on it. So, I'm going to approach Tegan. She owes you a favor."

"She can't overstep the elders, Kai."

"She won't think to if we don't at least ask."

He shouldn't let himself hope, but it was blooming in his chest anyway. Despite how awful he'd been, his parents were still fighting for him.

# NIGHT IS DARKEST
# BEFORE DAWN

## CHAPTER 7
# TRAINING

"E aon!"

Flinching, Eaon ducked his head and looked over his shoulder. Since officially graduating from his secondary educations a couple of weeks ago, his days were now filled solely with laborer training. The call had come from Ilwyn's office, which could only mean he was in trouble again. For what reason, he couldn't guess. Nothing he did was ever right.

Leaving the scrubbing brush and bucket with Meenis, who glared as if it was his fault he was being called away, Eaon hurried to the new Head of House.

Ilwyn was so distantly related to Eaon he didn't have a way to describe it, but when the last Head of House had been chosen by the Lover, Ilwyn had taken on the mantel. She had settled into the big office easily, and when Eaon arrived, she was not alone.

A male he didn't know was sitting across from her, leaning back in his chair with hands behind his head, ankles crossed, bare feet on the desk. Clearly he was of some importance to sit with such disrespect in the Nemuse home.

Ilwyn didn't look up from where she was writing as she barked, "Go stand in the corner."

Eaon frowned but didn't question the command. Moving to the nearest corner, he stood and waited.

"Face to the wall," she continued with a sigh, as if his lack of mind-reading skills annoyed her.

Eaon ground his teeth as he turned around to stare at the wall. He was sick to death of these power plays. These humiliations she kept coming up with for him. The silence lingered for a moment before the two witches began discussing plans for someone's birthday party, as if he wasn't even there. Ridiculous.

But things could be worse, and because of that, he endured it.

Thanks to his ma's begging, the Head of House had not sent him to live at the labor camps at the soonest opportunity. While he still had morning tertiary classes there, he had been allowed to stay home where Ellissa could brew his tonics and heal his injuries. Where his da was more regularly staying behind to keep him company, even though it meant he labored as well. Where he could watch his little sister growing up, fourteen now and coming into her own. Such an incredible blessing bloomed inside her, and Eaon had long since gotten a handle on his jealousy over it. The words his mind spat every time she spoke, every time she performed magic—arrogant, naive, selfish—he had replaced with alternatives—confident, happy, carefree. She did not suffer the way he suffered, and for that Eaon was glad.

However, she was not flawless. Like Dearmead, she struggled with the more academic side of her studies. While Dea had never gotten a strong grip on reading and writing, Eavha's attention was easily stolen away. She missed a lot of what was discussed in class and her grades were slipping because of it.

So most days, after they had their separate dinners, Eavha would join him at the round dining table and he helped her study. Maybe Eaon couldn't be a part of the family, couldn't be useful, couldn't contribute to the clan, but he could certainly make sure Eavha had the best chance of having a good life. Even if their Head of House didn't like his interfering with the family prodigy. Even if it meant the occasional beating with a broomstick, many of which had snapped over his back and left him riddled with splinters. He could and would handle it.

For hours, he stood as still as he could in the corner of Ilwyn's office, worried that shifting his weight too often would result in a scolding. He recited one of his favorite books to himself by memory alone, planning how he would read it aloud to Dearmead later. Dea wouldn't admit it, but Eaon knew he enjoyed the dramatic retellings more than anything else they got up to together in their cave behind the waterfall.

"You can go now," Ilwyn said.

Eaon blinked, waiting for the guest to leave.

"Eaon, I'm talking to you. Go."

Practically sagging in relief, he rushed from the room.

Pointless. Absolute waste of his time.

Meenis had finished the scrubbing on his own and was no doubt complaining to the others about how Eaon had abandoned him again. He had given up at this point on trying to make friends with the other laborers. To them, he would always be a Nemuse. And to his family, he would always be nothing.

Sitting at the dinner table with Kailevi, Eaon turned his porridge in its bowl, too tired to bother eating it.

"You alright?" Kailevi asked, the same worried note in his voice that he always had these days.

"Yes, Da. I'm fine. Just another shitty day."

More to soothe Kailevi's worries than to satiate a non-existent appetite, Eaon forced himself to take a bite.

"What happened?"

From the dining room, raucous laughter broke out. Eaon looked over his shoulder at the door, wondering if they were laughing at him.

"Just the same old crap," Eaon sighed, forcing another bite.

"Like what?"

Eaon rolled his eyes. "Why do you ask? It only pisses you off."

"Because I don't want you to have to bear it alone. Talk to me."

"Honestly, it's nothing. Ilwyn made me stand in her office while she was talking to some male for a few hours. It was stupid and pointless. I don't know what was so entertaining about having me waste my time staring at the wall."

Kailevi froze.

"Who was she in the room with?" he asked, voice cracking.

"I don't know." Eaon shrugged, pushing the rest of his dinner away. "And I don't care. Meenis is pissed at me and will probably make me do all the worst jobs tomorrow. I need to get to bed."

Kailevi nodded, but his neck was reddening, his fist clenching around his spoon. An utter overreaction that Eaon didn't have the energy to deal with.

As he left the table and stepped into the hall, he heard Kailevi get out of his chair. Waiting, thinking his da had thought of something to say to him, Eaon turned back toward the kitchen. But Kailevi wasn't coming after him. He was heading for the dining hall.

Groaning, Eaon shook his head. He could hear the shouting start as he shut himself in his room, peeled off the day's clothes and collapsed in bed.

---

When morning classes at the labor camps finished the next day and his teacher called for him to remain behind, Eaon bristled. He had limited time before he had to start work at home, and every minute he was delayed was a minute he didn't get to spend at lunch with Dearmead.

"I spoke with your Head of House this morning," his teacher told him, leaning against the desk and plucking a piece of paper from their desk.

"Oh?"

"Yes. She would like you to begin extra training."

Eaon sagged. "Oh."

"You should feel proud, Eaon. Normally we wait until witches are older to move on to the next stage, but you show potential. Do well, and your family will be proud of you."

He seriously doubted that.

"Here, take these directions to Teacher Hillis's house. He will oversee your training."

"Now?"

"Yes, now." His teacher gave him a withering look.

Bowing deeply, Eaon took the directions and his satchel and went to find Teacher Hillis.

---

He shouldn't have been so surprised to find the male from Ilwyn's office opening the door. Now that he wasn't reclining in Ilwyn's office, Eaon had to crane his neck to look at him, though doing so at all was rude.

"Good. You're on time. Come in."

Eaon bowed deeply before entering, looking around the house. It was smaller than any Eaon had ever seen, meaning Teacher Hillis did not come from a large family. Hardly any, judging by the state of things. Without a large family he would not be entitled to a laborer to help keep house, and it was clear that Teacher Hillis didn't do much himself.

*"With root and twine, be locked,"* Hillis muttered, a hand on the door. Magic swelled, and Eaon felt the air tingle as a spell locked the house.

Heart pounding, Eaon dropped his bag. Hillis held up his hands and smiled.

"Don't fret. I get many visitors and I don't want to be disturbed during your training," he explained.

Itching to ask what training, exactly, he was to undertake, Eaon bit the inside of his cheek and tried to calm himself down. Thinking of Ilwyn's broom again kept him silent.

"Good," Teach Hillis said, giving Eaon a slow appraisal. "You're eighteen, correct? Tall for your age, and filling out nicely. Getting much attention from females yet?"

Eaon blinked. "What?"

"Even the low-blessed females have needs. You'd make an enjoyable partner, I think. Or is it males for you? Doesn't matter, really."

Eaon felt the heat in his cheeks and hated it. Refused to answer. Like Hillis had said, it didn't matter.

"You'll train with me first, then with my wife Retty. We'll

alternate until you're perfect," Hillis said, going to draw the blinds on the windows.

He couldn't help it. The question slipped out. "At what?"

Hillis raised his eyebrows. "I was told you were smart."

"I . . ."

"Sex, Eaon. Ilwyn wants you trained for her and her husband. You're here to learn how to be useful in every way you will need to be if you expect anyone to provide for you."

The word hit him in the gut harder than any blow.

"No. I'm not going to do that. No. No." He couldn't stop saying it, even as he reached to pick up his satchel.

This was where he drew the line. He'd take the beating when he got home.

"It's not an optional component of your training," Teacher Hillis said, crossing his arms.

Eaon didn't care. "Unlock the door."

Never before had he wished so deeply to be blessed. To have enough magic to unlock it himself.

"Don't make this difficult. I have some papaver and some wine to calm you down if you need it."

"Go fuck yourself," Eaon hissed, pulling at the door that would not budge. "I'm not doing this and you can't make me."

"I can and I will. Now take your clothes off, I'll get you a drink."

Hillis went to the kitchen. Eaon gave up on the door and went to the window, pulling back the drapes. But it was not the kind of window that opened, and when he slammed his heavy satchel against the glass, magic bounced it back. Desperately, he searched for someone—anyone—he could wave down for help. But Hillis's house was remote, and there was nobody close enough to see him.

Trying to slow his steadily quickening breaths, Eaon looked for another way out.

The roof.

The hatching was not in the best shape, and he was strong enough to break it if he could get up there.

There wasn't time.

Hillis came back in with a bottle of wine and a pipe stuffed with papaver.

"Come on. Here."

Eaon clutched his bag tighter, holding it over his shoulder. There were enough books in there to do serious damage if he could get the right swing.

"Last chance before we do this the hard way," Hillis warned him, eyes darkening. "I know you know how to do what you're told. You passed the test yesterday perfectly."

Eaon braced himself, but the simmering anger in Kailevi's face when Eaon had told him what Ilwyn had made him do, the fighting he'd only heard the beginnings of last night . . . had his da known what the test was for? Had he let Eaon go to school this morning, knowing what was going to happen?

The thoughts emptied out of his head as Hillis slammed a hand on the table and stomped across the floor toward him. Eaon swung his bag, but Hillis blocked it with his forearm. Still, it must have hurt, because he stumbled. Eaon hit him again, aiming for his head, but Hillis charged before he could connect. Slamming Eaon against the wall, Hillis tore the satchel from his hands and tossed it on the floor, grabbing a fistful of the hair on the top of his head in one fist and wrapping the other around his throat.

"This could—" Hillis started, but Eaon's clenched fist flew into his chin.

Hillis must have had experience being fought like this,

because he didn't let go of Eaon, tightening his grip until Eaon could barely breathe. Ignoring the shattering pain lancing through his hand, Eaon hit the male again. Anywhere he could reach, again and again in a desperate attack that sparked a little fear in Hillis's eyes as he struggled to control Eaon.

His grip loosened just enough to give Eaon room to bring a knee up between Hillis's legs. Hard.

Gasping, Hillis's knees weakened and he finally let go.

Grabbing the bottle of wine, Eaon bashed him over the head with it. The glass shattered and the little cabin trembled with the force of Hillis's frame collapsing to the ground.

Eaon couldn't tell if the stain growing on the wooden floor was wine or blood or both.

Had he just killed someone?

He almost didn't care.

Breaths coming too hard and too fast, Eaon dragged the dining table to the lowest part of the ceiling, climbed atop it, then lifted a chair over his head and broke apart the thatching. He had no thoughts, no emotion, nothing except adrenaline numbing the pain in his hands as he placed the chair atop the table, climbed on it, and hauled himself onto the ceiling beam.

There was no good way to get down once he was outside. Gripping the edge of the roof, he tried to lower himself down as best he could, but his injured hands couldn't take his weight and he dropped.

He heard his ankle crack as he landed, and the scream that tore out of him was half pain and half frustration.

Nobody was nearby enough to hear him.

Getting up, all he knew was that he needed to get away. Needed to get somewhere safe.

He limped as fast as he could toward the nearby river.

CHAPTER 8

# BREAKING

It was late when Dearmead returned to his room, stripped out of his clothes and climbed into bed, exhausted from the extended training he'd done with his cousin after classes. His body ached from the numerous fights he had lost, bruises already discoloring his arms, back and chest.

Just as he let out a heavy sigh, there was a tap on his window.

Groaning deeply, he realized he'd forgotten to send a whispering leaf to Eaon about the late training session. No doubt he'd be pissed at him for not showing up to the waterfall.

Getting out of bed, Dearmead went and pushed open his shutters.

Eavha stood there in her night gown, brown eyes wide and red, cheeks stained with dried tears. Looking around the gardens, it was clear she was alone. Even more surprisingly, the guardians on patrol hadn't spotted her.

"Eavha, what are you doing?" he asked, voice heavy with concern. "What's wrong?"

"Eaon's missing. He didn't come home. Is he here?"

"What?" Dearmead frowned. "No. Are you sure—"

"Everybody is furious that he hasn't shown up. They're threatening to disown him. Ma and Da have been out searching for him all night, sending him whispering leaves and trying to follow them, but the magic keeps failing. Which is scaring them. He could be dead, Dearmead. They don't know why else the leaves would do that. Please. Please tell me he's here."

Dearmead couldn't breathe. "Eavha, go home. I'll find him."

"I want to come with you."

"Go home before your parents realize you're gone too. You'll give them a heart attack. I promise you, I will find him."

He was already halfway out the window, not bothering to put on a shirt first.

"You promise?"

"I promise."

Sagging with relief, Eavha nodded and began to hurry home.

Dearmead started running. Sick to his stomach, he knew where to look first.

---

Drenched, Dearmead stepped out of the waterfall and into the little cave, breathless from the run.

"Oh, thank the Mother," he panted.

Eaon was lying on his side, back to the waterfall. He didn't turn, and the sick feeling came back to Dearmead's stomach. Stilling, he listened for a breath, only drawing one himself when saw the shallow rise and fall of Eaon's shoulders.

"Eaon? What's wrong?"

Moving to Eaon's side, he crouched beside him. Which is

when he noticed the state of Eaon's hands. The bruises around his neck. The vacant look in his eyes as he stared at the wall.

"Fuck. What happened?"

"You weren't here," he whispered, and the lack of life in his voice only worsened the panic squeezing Dearmead's heart.

"I'm sorry. I had extra training during lunch and after class. Eaon, what happened? Who did this? Your Head of House?"

Though that didn't make sense if his Head of House was looking for him, too.

Eaon didn't answer. Gently, in case he was hurt, Dearmead placed a hand on Eaon's shoulder.

"Don't," he snarled, flinching away.

He'd been beaten before, Dearmead knew, and never had he reacted like this. The word was a threat, his whole body stiffening, readying for a fight. He'd *been* in a fight. Eaon would not have fought back against his Head of House, or any of his family, but he had fought back today.

"Eaon," Dearmead said again, hands shaking as ideas about what might have happened began to swirl in his head. He knew the quiet jokes people made about laborers. Knew they weren't always jokes. "Eaon . . ."

He couldn't ask, but he sat down properly and took deep, calming breaths.

He was going to kill someone.

"Eaon," he couldn't stop saying his name. "I need to tell your parents—"

"No!" Eaon snapped, sitting up suddenly with a wild hatred in his eyes.

"They think you're dead, Eaon."

He scoffed. "I wish."

"Don't."

"I'd rather be dead than be a laborer for one more minute,"

he spat. "I'd rather be thrown out of this clan. I hate them. I hate all of them. I hate my parents. I wish they were dead. I hope when they pass, they rot in the void forever."

"I'm sorry," Dearmead said, dropping his shoulders. He didn't know what else to say. Didn't know what to do. "I'm sorry. If you tell me who did this, I will break every fucking bone in their body until no healer in the world can put them back together again. I swear it."

The promise took some of the wind out of Eaon's sails. Took enough that he slumped against the wall and closed his eyes. "I might have killed him."

Dearmead blinked, his heart skipping a beat. "Good."

Eaon swallowed. "It wasn't . . . It wasn't, you know. I'm alright."

He was not alright. Regardless of how far things got, Eaon never should have been put in that position to begin with. None of the laborers should be. He thought of all the witches working in his house, for his family, and tried not to imagine how many of them had suffered at the hands of one of his cousins. His brothers and sisters.

"My parents think I'm dead?" Eaon asked as he peeled open his weary eyes, as if Dearmead's earlier words only now registered.

"They've been trying to send you whispering leaves all evening, but the magic, I don't know, it's not working or something. Eavha didn't explain well."

"Eavha?" Eaon sat up straighter. "What . . . Is she . . . I—"

"She's fine, she's fine. She came to get me when nobody could find you."

Eaon slumped back again, releasing a shaking breath.

"I should at least tell them you're not dead," Dearmead tried again.

Eyes closing once again, Eaon nodded. But his wrecked hands started shaking. "I can't go back. I can't. I can't do this anymore, Dea."

"Alright. Okay. You don't have to, okay?" He didn't know how he was going to keep that promise, but he would. "Just . . . wait here. Let me get some things. Some food and blankets and stuff. Something for your hands. I'll bring it here, and we'll just . . . stay here for a while."

Eaon scrunched his face, trying to hold back tears. Figuring he wanted some privacy, Dearmead left the waterfall.

Eaon was going to be furious, but he returned with more than just supplies.

"Oh, Eaon," Ellissa cried when she came through the waterfall.

Still cradling his broken hands, Eaon had buried his head in his knees and was openly sobbing. It only got worse at the sound of his mother's voice.

Dearmead put the blankets and food down and watched as Ellissa crouched beside her son. Taking one hand in her own, spell barely a breath on her lips, healing magic swelled in the cave until Dearmead felt a little ill. Sitting down to stop the dizziness, he watched Ellissa take Eaon's other hand, then his ankle, before placing her herb-stained hands on his neck.

The way Eaon flinched at the touch cut deep into Dearmead's own throat.

"Everything's going to be okay," Ellissa promised.

"No it's fucking not!" Eaon snapped, raising his head. "You and Da knew, didn't you? You knew, and you did nothing!"

Dearmead stepped back, eyes widening. But Ellissa was shaking her head.

"We did not do nothing, Eaon."

"You sent me off to camp—"

"We thought you'd be safe there! Kailevi and I spent all day at the Elder Traveler's camp petitioning for your da to be allowed to mentor. For you to be allowed to travel."

A spark of hope bloomed, quickly drowned by the anger back in Eaon's pained gaze. "Why didn't you warn me? You could have told me."

"There's a lot of things your da and I don't tell you, Eaon, because you don't need to know. We love you, and we have always been doing our best to protect you. You and your sister. I know . . . I know sometimes it might seem like we're sacrificing you to protect Eavha, but—"

"No, I know. I know why we have to stay." His voice broke, throat bobbing madly against the faint yellow marks still left behind. "But I can't anymore, Ma. I can't."

"I know. We're going to get this sorted out, okay? I'm going to get you out of here if it's the last thing I do, because, damn it, over my dead body will anybody hurt my children like that. Over my dead fucking body."

Eaon and Dearmead both balked at Ellissa's language. She hugged him then, and the alarm smothering every other emotion Eaon was drowning in was clue enough to how rare such an act of affection from his ma truly was. Eaon buried his head in her shoulder.

"Stay here for a while, okay?" Ellissa finally said, voice hoarse. "I'll come and get you when it's safe."

"Alright."

Ellissa left, and Dearmead handed Eaon a sandwich and blanket. Eaon wiped his face on the back of his sleeve and inspected the snack in his hands. The right one was still bruised, but whatever deeper damage had been done was healed.

"Thank you for getting her," he said. "I'm sorry I yelled at you before."

"Don't apologize," Dearmead said, shaking his head.

Carefully, he reached for Eaon's hand.

When he didn't pull away again, Dearmead raised it, curling Eaon's fingers in and placing his thumb on top. "If you're going to punch someone, make sure you hold your fist like this."

Eaon stared at their hands for a moment before nodding. Dearmead tapped his index and middle knuckles. "And try to use these as much as you can. It will still hurt, but you shouldn't break your hand quite as easily."

Eaon nodded again and Dearmead let him go. There was a faraway look in his eyes for a moment, his chest rising and falling too quickly. "What else?"

"What?"

"What else can you teach me?"

Dearmead found himself smiling.

For the first time, he was glad he had been trained to fight. Glad to be able to pass that knowledge on to someone who needed it.

***

"Dearmead, wake up," Eaon croaked.

The endless pummeling of the waterfall in the pool below had taken Dearmead into a deeper sleep than he'd expected to have after such an awful night, and every part of him was still heavy with it. "No."

"It's almost sunrise. Your ma will kill you if she finds you not at home."

That was enough to make him sit up. Eaon was lying on his side, blanket rolled up under his head as he rubbed at his weary eyes. It was unclear if he'd slept at all, and the emptiness had settled back in.

"What are you going to do today?"

Eaon shrugged. "Wait here."

By himself. When last night he'd said he wanted to die.

"I'll wait with you."

"You can't."

"Watch me."

"Your ma—"

"Can suck an egg."

Eaon snorted, a hint of life in his eyes again. Dearmead grinned and pointed to the basket of food and other things he had brought last night.

"I packed *The Battle for the Boab* last night. It's in the pile."

"Of course you did," Eaon said as he reached across and dragged the basket closer. "For someone who whinges so much about fighting, you have an obsession with war-related books."

"Bite me."

"You want me to bite you or read to you? I can't do both?"

It was such a relief to hear Eaon like himself that Dearmead chuckled. As dawn lit up the cave in flickering turquoise, the scent of peppercorn and jasmine permeating the air, Dearmead rolled onto his back and tucked his arms under his head.

"Read."

# CHAPTER 9

# TRAVELER

The first step Eaon took outside of Wyldeden didn't feel real. So he took another, craning his neck as he looked around at the mountainous trees surrounding them. Kailevi stood back, watching him carefully with two traveler's packs in his hands. A strong breeze blew between the redwood trunks and Eaon scuttled back, gasping.

"Was that wind?"

"Sure was," Kailevi said, smiling tightly. "How are you doing?"

He had been warned that stepping outside the Boab could be overwhelming. Warned that it was dangerous and hostile and that he was to stick to Kailevi's side like a limpet the whole time, or else this little experiment was over and he would have to go to the camps.

"It . . . smells different." Damper. Denser. The Anfar forest had a weight to it, a haze that dulled the sunlight filtering through the gray canopy far, far overhead. The ground was sharp and cold beneath his feet as he ground his toes into it, his fingernails already tinged with blue as he rubbed the gooseflesh dimpling his arms. "What season is it?"

"Mid autumn," Kailevi said, putting the pack down to remove a wool cloak. After draping it over Eaon's shoulders, Kailevi walked to a nearby shrub and rubbed the reddish-brown leaves. "See the coloring?"

Eaon's eyes widened. "It's not green."

"No. The leaves will change and wilt, and by winter the branches will be bare."

A cycle, he remembered. Come spring, the dead came back to life, but knowing and seeing were two very different things. Stepping forward, he winced and pulled his foot back as something sharp dug into his foot.

"Careful," Kailevi left the bush and went to inspect the red spot where the skin hadn't quite broken. "No healers out here if you get injured."

"How . . . how do you walk?" Eaon asked, realizing how many twigs and thorny stems lay drying on the ground. He couldn't possibly avoid them all.

Of course, if Terra had blessed him with more than a passing breath, the ground would have cleared and softened for him. When the Nemuse witches old enough to attend burials came out, they likely didn't have to think twice about it.

His chest squeezed. He wasn't going to be able to do this. The eagerness with which his ma had seen him off, practically pushing him through the portal into Anfar, would wilt like the leaves on the trees. He was going to fail—again. Thrown back into the camps and forced to—

"Hey, hey. Stop." Kailevi grabbed the edges of Eaon's cloak and pulled them tighter. "I'm not blessed either, remember? If I can do it, so can you."

Right. His exhale shook as he let it loose.

"I couldn't say it in there in case someone overheard," Kailevi whispered, scowling at the witch mark carved over the fold in the Boab. "But magic doesn't make a witch, Eaon. It's your heart, your devotion to the Spirits, that counts. Be strong in here"—Kailevi put a hand on Eaon's chest—"and the earth will listen."

"But—"

"Trust me."

But he wasn't strong. Not in his heart, not anywhere. Closing his eyes against another buffeting breeze, Eaon swayed. That tiny, pathetic kernel of magic that sputtered fruitlessly inside him was the only anchor he had to the world, and it reached desperately back for the Boab.

"One step," Kailevi encouraged, holding onto Eaon's elbow.

He had to try.

No, he had to *do* this. Because if he didn't, he had to go back.

He stepped forward, wincing again as small bits of loose bark bit his feet. A twig snapped loudly and the forest seemed to groan in response.

"This is not Wyldeden," Kailevi said, guiding him forward another step. "This is Anfar. This is where your people truly belong. It is Mother's realm, not Terra's, and we are all Mother's creatures. We are all equal in her eyes."

"All of nature is—"

"Don't recite your textbook to me right now. I know all of nature is Terra's domain. But she is a caretaker in Mother's garden, and she does not watch you now. So walk."

He did, each footstep somehow noisier than the last.

But Kailevi's words ran through his head, over and over. Anfar was not Wyldeden. That much was blatantly clear. Opening his eyes, he took a good look at this new world open to him. Every twisted root dipping in and out of the ground like a man-sized worm, the pungent moss that grew on it. Somewhere deep in the gloom ahead, the cry of an animal he had never heard before was almost drowned out by the groaning wood and whistling leaves. He could have sworn a knot in the trunk of a nearby trunk shifted slightly to watch him.

"Keep going," Kailevi whispered, eyes scanning ahead. "It's just a nosy dryad."

Eaon swallowed. There were certainly no dryads in Wyldeden. A fae so intrinsically part of the tree that not even the wards around Anfar could expel them. Symbiotic, the way witches were meant to be with their blessings. With the Spirits. One and the same.

But not him. At least not with Terra or Sanni or Jem, or any of the other elemental spirits he'd learned about in school. But Kailevi was right about that, too; he was still Mother's creature. He had as much right to be here as the dryads and the trees and whatever it is that howled deep in the wild.

His next step fell silently. As did every step after that.

CHAPTER 10

# LEATHER

Dearmead watched the Boab and counted the days until Eaon returned.

Even when he really shouldn't have been.

The guardian's staff hit him in the shoulder, then in the same breath twirled around and hit his side. He hissed at the contact that stung the bruises already blooming across his skin beneath the leather. The other junior guardians watching the match laughed at his expense, but Calla didn't join them. His ma stood at the top of the rise with the other senior guardians, assessing the fresh crop joining the ranks. The exact tone of her disapproval and the words she would say later, *"How dare you embarrass our family name with such poor performance,"* already rang in his ears.

But he found he no longer cared if he embarrassed her. Not after watching her the last few days and realizing there was a laborer in their house she had set her sights on. That joined her and his da in their bedroom at night and only left in the morning, red eyed and shaking.

As the guardian in the ring with him spun, whipping his staff low to knock Dearmead's legs out from under him, he pulled his gaze from the Boab to his ma and jumped over it. Teeth bared, he swung his own training staff and caught the guardian in the face. The crowd cried out in a sympathetic groan as blood spattered across the dirt, but the match was not over yet.

Dearmead kept one eye on his opponent and one eye on his ma. Making sure she knew he was thinking about her when he blocked the volley of blows his opponent attempted. That he was imagining it was her when he caught an opening in his opponent's defenses again and jabbed the end of his staff into their stomach, then brought the length of his staff down on their shoulder. The crack of their collarbone could be heard through the valley, but still, this wasn't over. Even as the other guardian looked up at him from where they had dropped to one knee, bitter respect in their eyes, they did not concede.

One armed, the guardian tried to block Dearmead's blows but it was hardly an effort to disarm them now. That they still didn't concede gave Dearmead cause to nod his respect in return.

Calla would want him to beat this guardian senseless. To take his staff and bring it down on them until the pain forced them to tap out. Bayfields did not show mercy. Bayfields were the alphas among the guardian ranks. But it was not his opponent's fault that they had been matched today, and so Dearmead made sure his ma was watching as he delivered a single jab of his staff to the neck and forced his opponent to pass out.

The gathered witches crowed and applauded, making way for the elder guardian. Dearmead put down his training staff and bowed deeply.

"Congratulations, Dearmead Bayfield. You may officially join the ranks of our junior guardians."

Keeping his head down, he raised his hands like he had been instructed to do and let the elder place the branch of ironwood in them.

"Your staff, to become an extension of your own body. Of your soul."

"Thank you, Elder."

He stood, inspecting the raw branch. He would spend the next few months carving it until it was perfect. Every scrape of the knife, every pass of the sharpening stone, would be done with Terra's blessing pulsing through his veins, strengthening the wood and leaving a piece of himself in it so that it would respond best to only him.

Despite his victory, Calla did not look happy. Dearmead leveled his own glare back as he left the training ring. His opponent would be taken to the healer's clinic, and when they were able they would have to fight again. Again and again, until they won.

***

"Hey, Dearmead!" One of his many cousins and a few of her friends jogged to where Dearmead had perched at the top of hill where he could see the Boab.

"What?" He was not interested in whatever she had to say.

As soon as he had been able to find a place to be alone, the breaking bones and splattering blood rang in his ears, churning his stomach until he'd been violently ill. He was still nauseous and not in the mood for company.

"A few of us are organizing a little bonfire tonight to start our carvings," she explained, twirling her own branch across her shoulder. "Want to join?"

"Not really."

He had sent a whispering leaf with a messenger for Eaon, to let him know he had passed his trials today. Without knowing how far from Wyldeden they had already traveled, there was no way to know how long it would take to hear back, but he waited anyway.

"It's going to be a real party," his cousin continued. "We invited some gardeners to come and they're bringing wine. A few others, too. Pretty witches who were practically drooling over us today."

Her friends chuckled.

"Not. Interested."

And it was true. The idea of spending time or having the attention of anyone else was utterly uninteresting. When had he become so addicted to Eaon's company?

"Suit yourself." His cousin shrugged, muttering under her breath as the group of them walked away. Her friends laughed again, but he didn't care.

Didn't care about much of anything as he trudged home, passing the clearing his cousin and her friends had begun to build the bonfire in. A familiar flash of mousy hair caught his eye and he stilled. But of course it wasn't Eaon. Eaon wasn't here. Even if he was, there was no way he'd be invited to a party, nor would he want to go.

But the color and curls had caught his attention for a reason. Bundled up on her head, loose tendrils spilling down her neck, Eavha was among those keenly listening to one of the new guardians' stories.

It would make sense that she was invited, even if she was far too young to be drinking wine. She was pretty and high caliber and, if a witch was willing to wait a few years, they would be hard pressed to find a better partner to breed with.

His stomach churned again and he found himself marching down the hall into the clearing.

"Dearmead!" His cousin called, waving at him. "Changed your mind?"

"Apparently."

Eavha's head snapped up at the sound of his name, a huge grin breaking across her face. He grimaced as he headed toward the patch of grass where she and a few others had settled. The blond witch sitting quietly beside Eavha was also popular; Apaete was making a name for herself as a talented healer, and her timid nature was well suited to counter Eavha's boldness.

"Hey, Dea," Eavha said as he sat down beside her. "Congratulations on passing your trials."

"Thanks." Placing his branch down, he turned to give the other male guardian a withering look.

That was all it took for the color to drain from his face. "I'll . . . go talk to Annae."

"Good idea," Dearmead practically growled as the male got up and left. He supposed being a Bayfield did have its perks.

Once they were alone, he turned to Eavha.

"Does your ma know you're here?"

"She's on night shift at the clinic." She avoided answering, twirling a loose curl around her finger.

Dearmead sighed. "This isn't really a party you should be at." He turned to Apaete, whose cheeks were reddening quickly. "Either of you."

"We were invited," Apaete said bashfully, hands folded in the gauzy skirt all the female healers wore, slit up the sides so her pale leg was on display. "And we weren't going to drink."

"Oh, please let us stay, Dea. I don't want to go home by myself."

He sighed again. Deeply. Because that was a sentiment he understood too well.

"Fine," he said. "I'll get something for you both to drink."

"And then will you tell us about your match?" Eavha asked, eyes widening, long lashes fluttering. Apaete was no better, ducking her head and somehow finding an even darker shade of red to turn.

Lover take him.

"Only if you tell me about what you guys have been up to in the healer's college," he countered, hoping he could get them to do most of the talking.

———

Two weeks.

Fourteen days and six hours after leaving Nir, Eaon came back through the Boab. Dearmead overheard the news from guardians gossiping in the halls of the training center and was fidgeting through the rest of his classes until he could finally leave.

He went to the Nemuse home first, but Ellissa told him Kailevi was reporting in with the elder and Eaon had gone for a walk. Which meant Dearmead knew exactly where to find him.

Through the bordering forest, it took him less than ten minutes to reach their waterfall. Leaping up the jutting stone steps, he jumped through the falling water and landed in a crouch.

Eaon was lounging with a book, but dropped it when Dearmead came barrelling in.

"You're back," Dearmead grinned.

"Don't remind me."

The sour note in his voice was mixed with something else that Dearmead couldn't identify, but the way Eaon's gaze roamed over him was a reminder that this would be the first time he was seeing Dearmead in his official guardian leathers.

"Did you get my leaf?" he asked.

"No." Eaon shook his head. "But I didn't doubt you'd pass. It suits you."

"What does?"

"The leather."

"It's still a bit stiff, but it'll loosen. And then there's this."

He grabbed his branch from where he'd left it in the cave, twirling it around to show off. He had whittled it down to the right size, but there was still a lot of work to do. Eaon glanced over it and gave him a smile.

"Congratulations."

"But what about you? How was it out there?" Dearmead sat beside him and reached for the basket he'd also left in the cave with a collection of stones and cutting tools inside. While the other junior guardians worked on their staffs at home or in the fields, Dearmead had preferred privacy.

"It was . . . different."

"Tell me."

For hours, Dearmead sat and worked on his staff while Eaon told him about Nir. About the whispering sentient trees and the dryads that lived inside them. The earth that was harsher than the ground in Wyldeden, but that he'd *finally* learned to walk silently on. The towering mountains, so much taller than he'd thought, like a wall of rock that one could climb all the way to the open sky where clouds and rain and fog descended from. He talked about the cold and the true sun, showing Dearmead the freckled skin on his shoulders where it had burned him.

Dearmead pressed a finger to Eaon's warm shoulder, the heat of it spreading down into his core. He wanted to lay his hand on the bare skin, to feel more of that heat fill him up, but Eaon was talking about the other witches he'd met, the faeries he'd seen dancing among the clovers, mushrooms growing from their heads.

Then there were the languages. There was more joy—more life—in Eaon's amber eyes than Dearmead had ever seen before as he talked about the languages, cultures and traditions of the small clan that lived at the base of the mountains bordering Anfar.

Dearmead listened to every word. And when his carving knife went dull, he put it aside and grabbed the spare. Eaon picked up the dull blade and a sharpening stone, still talking as he drew the knife in sharp, practiced jerks across the stone. Only Dearmead's staring made him pause.

"Am I doing it wrong?"

"No," Dearmead promised. "But you don't have to do that."

Sharpening stone into a blade was something he'd learned to do in case he was ever posted outside the Boab and needed to sharpen his weapons, but being a Bayfield meant that aside from initial classes, he'd never had to do it. There were plenty of laborers whose hands could bleed on his behalf.

"I don't mind," Eaon said, then frowned. "Unless you don't want me to. I know the process is meant to be personal—"

"No, I don't mind. I just didn't want you to think you had to. I can do it myself if you don't want to."

Eaon stared at him for a while, and again, Dearmead didn't understand the look on his face. Had never seen anyone look like that before. Something akin to pain, but laced with gratitude.

"I don't mind," he finally said. "Not for you."

CHAPTER II
# FATIGUE

For a while, the reaping of the Nemuse family normalized. Then on the night of the New Year, seven dropped dead for no apparent reason at all. The revel had ramped up a notch as they celebrated the honor the Lover had bestowed upon the family, but, for the first time, a number of Nemuses seemed to balk. Dearmead didn't blame them, barely able to pass on his congratulations with a straight face.

Ellissa knew. She'd shared a worried look with him as Dearmead gifted the family a bouquet of iridescent flowers at the funerals. Their numbers were dwindling quickly, and if this accelerated reaping didn't stop soon then it was only a matter of time before someone they cared about would be taken.

Kailevi needed to stay in Wyldeden for a while and Eaon wasn't old enough to travel alone, which meant he had to labor again. And every day that passed, Dearmead saw the life Nir had given back to Eaon fading away.

One day he went to the waterfall after training and found no sign that Eaon had been there at all. He didn't expect the panic.

The hot chills that prickled down his spine, the nausea turning his stomach or the sudden urgency to find him. Grabbing the freshly completed staff from where he'd left it in the cave, he ran back to the forest and all the way to the Nemuse house.

The arguing could be heard from across the dandelion field, and Dearmead's grip tightened on his staff as he raced to the door. Bursting into the kitchenette, he took in Kailevi standing in hall, blocking one of the other Nemuse witches from going down there. Both of them stopped at the sight of Dearmead, weapon in hand.

"Can I help you, Bayfield?" It was the new Head of House, he realized. Barely a week into the role.

"I'm looking for Eaon," Dearmead said stiffly, glancing to Kailevi.

That the male was putting himself in such a position—a low-blessed witch who would not submit to his Head of House—said all he needed to know about where Eaon was and why he had not come to the waterfall today.

"He's not well," Kailevi ground out through clenched teeth, leveling a glare at the Head. "And he needs to rest."

"He needs to do what he is told," the Head hissed back.

"I already said I would do his share of the chores."

"And I already said *no*. I've sent the last of the laborers back to the camps and I will send you as well if you don't move aside."

This is what it had come to. The Nemuse family was so small now they could not have additional laborers. Only Kailevi and Eaon, when they weren't traveling. And when they were . . . well, it was the head's responsibility to take care of the household. No wonder they were in such a rage, and Dearmead wondered if Eaon would be allowed to travel anymore at all, now that things had gotten so bad.

"Go, Dearmead," Kailevi said to him, jerking his head to the side.

"But—"

"I can handle this."

The Head of House's fists curled, but there was something in Kailevi's stance warning that he would not be moving aside anytime soon.

Dearmead backed out of the kitchenette, but he didn't go home. He jogged around the outside of the house to Eaon's bare window. He was in bed, pillow over his head.

Angling his staff through first, Dearmead clambered inside.

"Eaon."

The shouting from down the hall picked up again and Eaon stiffened beneath the blanket. At the threats coming from the Head of House, Dearmead understood why. And he understood why Kailevi would not let them down the hall. Whatever grace Eaon had been given in the past for his episodes was gone, this new Head promising to dope him up with enough stimulants to raise the dead if Eaon didn't get up and get to work soon. He didn't care that doing so would fry his brain. Would destroy Eaon's body from the inside out. Whatever it took to make the leech *useful*.

Taking a seat on the floor by Eaon's bed, he reached beneath the blanket and found Eaon's hand.

"You should see him out there," Dearmead said, squeezing tightly. "Your da would give my ma a run for the title of most intimidating witch in Wyldeden right now."

Eaon didn't laugh, hand limp in Dearmead's. Another flutter of panic forced him to suck down a sharp breath, before he pulled the pillow off Eaon's head. Not dead, but not really alive, either. His eyes were heavy lidded and shadowed, as if he hadn't slept in a year. He lay limp on the bed, breaths coming shallow and slow.

"Hey, are you okay?"

He seemed to notice Dearmead for the first time, blinking through the haze. "I'm tired."

The words were barely a breath.

"Did you take something? Do you have a tonic around?"

Eaon just stared. Dearmead had never seen him this bad before.

Swallowing the lump in his throat, keeping his staff nearby, Dearmead did the only thing he could think of. He picked up one of the many books scattered on the floor and opened it, forcing his brain to block out the shouting from down the hall and focus on the words. Slowly, he began to read aloud. And the next time he paused to look back at Eaon, his friend was watching.

———

Every day for the next week, Dearmead came to Eaon's room after training to read to him. Sometimes Ellissa was there, helping Eaon get some food down, or Eavha, healing a bruise nobody would tell Dearmead the origins of. Kailevi was often busy doing the work of two laborers, but he smiled at Dearmead when he saw him coming across the fields.

"It's helping," he took the time to tell him one day. "Your visits are helping."

Something certainly was, because Eaon was sitting up in bed when Dearmead came through the door. There was still an endless apathy in his eyes, but his mouth turned up in a half smile as Dearmead closed the door behind him.

"Hey. How are you doing?"

Eaon shrugged, turning to the window. "Better enough to feel guilty."

Dearmead sat on the bed and took Eaon's hand again, lacing their fingers together. "You have nothing to feel guilty about. This isn't your fault."

"I'm a burden on my family."

Dearmead shook his head. "They love you."

It took a moment, but Eaon took a shuddering breath before continuing. "Ma and Da have been talking about breeding again."

"Sounds about right." Dearmead had twenty-nine brothers and sisters. Eaon's parents were younger than Dearmead's, but it was still strange for them to not have had more witchlings.

"The Head wants Eavha to breed, too," Eaon continued.

"What?" Dearmead frowned. "Eavha's not even fifteen yet."

"That's what our parents said. But they're desperate. Desperate enough to want me to do it too."

Something slimy churned in Dearmead's stomach. "You're not fully grown yet either. And you shouldn't have to breed if you don't want to."

"I don't," Eaon admitted, red creeping up his neck. "Ma and Da know I don't. But they also know that if that's what needs to be done to save our family, then I'll do it. I'll do what I have to."

"That's not fair."

"What *is* fair?" Eaon countered. "It's how things are. At least here, anyway."

"You could go somewhere else," Dearmead found himself saying, startled again by the intensity of the panic building inside him. "You could go wild."

Eaon seemed to think about it, but then shook his head. "No, I have things to stay for."

Dearmead didn't imagine the way Eaon's gaze drifted to

him, then shot away again. Swallowing the lump in his throat, Dearmead dared to risk it.

"I could come with you."

Anything. Anything to keep Eaon to himself a little longer.

This time Eaon laughed, and Dearmead nearly cried at the relief that came from hearing it. He knew then that what he felt was more than friendship. He cared too much.

"I'm serious."

"Dea, neither of us would last an hour out there on our own."

"I don't know, I'm top of the class in my training."

Eaon looked at him then, a tiny scrap of hope coming to life. "Maybe one day."

One day. Dearmead made a silent promise that he would commit to his training more than he ever so that when "one day" came, he would be ready.

# IT BLOOMS IN THE THORNIEST PLACES

# CHAPTER 12
# HONOR

As the years went by, it didn't get easier to say goodbye to Eaon. When he was here, Dearmead caught himself memorizing the planes of his face, the different smiles he had, the way his body moved when he dove from their cave beneath the waterfall, swimming together in the pool beneath for hours. And when he was gone, Dearmead forced his mind to replicate those details. To picture Eaon so clearly he could almost pretend he was in the room with him.

It had been four months since he'd last seen him. During the summer, none of the other travelers wanted to travel north, so Kailevi was left with the job. And Eaon, as always, jumped on any opportunity to get out of the Boab again. Which was fair, and Dearmead was always glad for Eaon that he could get away. Was glad the traveling made him happy. But he missed him. More and more each time.

Dearmead mulled over it as he flicked blueberries across his plate, only half listening to the chatter around him at the breakfast table. His pathetic aching was only interrupted when a familiar name pricked his ears.

He sat up straight, turning to one of his distantly related cousins down the table. "What did you say?"

"When?" she asked, shoveling mango and yogurt into her mouth.

"Just now. About the Nemuses."

"Oh." She shrugged, clearly distantly related enough not to know how much the name meant to him. "Lana gets to come back in the Boab today because the Nemuse travelers finally returned from the North Mountains—"

Dearmead didn't wait to finish listening, jumping from his seat and leaving his breakfast. His braid swung behind him as he ran through the halls and out the door, ignoring the indignant shouts of those he pushed past as he raced up the hills toward the lake. All those drills, all those vomit-inducing workouts up and down the steepest hills in Wyldeden, had been worth it for the extra seconds of speed he gained as he went in search of Eaon.

Twisting through the inner city paths, dodging laborers carrying wares, barrelling past the makers and the farmers offering their goods, he didn't stop until he reached the temples. Beyond them lay the perfect blue of the lake and the bridge pulled taut between the Boab's island and the shore.

Kailevi and Eaon had just finished crossing, clothes ragged and filthy from the long weeks of travel. Their heavy packs hit the ground and Eaon turned his face to the sun, linking his hands behind his back and stretching his shoulders. Thinner than he had been before he left, and yet somehow stronger, too. Lean muscle corded along his arms, his calves toned as he lifted one foot to rub the soles of his blackened feet.

Kailevi spotted Dearmead first and smiled, saying something

to Eaon, whose head snapped around faster than a whip. The grin that broke across his face made Dearmead smile too.

Jogging the last dozen meters, Dearmead took the traveler's packs for them.

"Welcome home."

The smile on Eaon's face faltered.

"Hello, Dearmead," Kailevi said. "Are you busy? Would you mind taking those? This last week has been rough."

"Of course, what happened?" Dearmead asked, falling into step beside them as they headed toward the traveler's station.

"A little territory war between a wild forest coven and a rogue witch," Eaon said, eyes lighting up. "We accidentally stumbled into the middle of it and had to make a run for the Boab."

Dearmead's heart leaped into his throat. "Are you alright?"

"We're fine," Kailevi promised. "But I'll be spending some time with the elder to start another petition. We need guardians to accompany travelers on our missions."

Eaon snorted, but didn't say what Dearmead knew he was thinking. For a petition like that to go through, the high priestess would have to approve it. So would the elder guardian, who'd then have to re-organize the entire faction to reassign people. Neither of them cared enough about travelers to risk it.

"I would sign it," Dearmead said, shuffling Eaon's pack into a more comfortable position on his shoulder. "Without travelers, our relations with other clans would be in ribbons. You should be protected."

"Or at least trained," Kailevi said with a nod. "Without magic, we should at least be given training to defend ourselves."

Dearmead looked to Eaon, who was too deep in his own head to listen to the conversation.

"Thank you, Dearmead," Kailevi added once they reached

the travelers' station, taking both packs. By the depth in the male's eyes and the gravel in his voice, Dearmead knew it was for more than carrying their packs he was being thanked for. "You two go. I'll meet you back home."

"Sure," Eaon said, blinking the daze out of his eyes. Turning to Dearmead, a spark of mischief lit up his face. "I have stuff to tell you."

Dearmead nodded, eager for Eaon's stories. Even the ones that terrified him, the ones that made Nir sound like a cesspool of vicious madness, Dearmead loved listening to every detail, every word.

They went to their waterfall and sat on a boulder half submerged in the pool at the bottom. Dipping his filthy feet into the water, Eaon moaned in relief.

"The North Mountains are far," Dearmead said, sliding his feet in as well and wriggling his toes in the tepid pool. The cacophony of plummeting water nearby masked their conversation, the spray of the cascade leaving droplets of crystals on their faces.

"The only place more of a pain to get to is the wastes in Bernt," Eaon agreed, running his long fingers through his hair, shaking out loose leaves that had been stuck in there for Mother knew how long.

As they sat, Dearmead sent a whispering leaf to his senior pretending he was ill, preferring to listen to Eaon's adventures. For an hour, he watched Eaon untangle his hair, clean it, then wash his feet and face until he no longer looked like a wild witch, all while telling Dearmead about the walk to the North Mountains. About the clan that had settled there, mostly Terra-blessed but with a large portion of dual-blessed Ignatius witches too.

"I made a . . . friend," Eaon said, laying back on the rock and gazing at the wispy clouds high above as the sun dried his mousy brown locks.

"Yeah?"

"His name is Tomaii. Mother shield me, Dea, we got in so much trouble."

Dearmead laughed. "That doesn't sound like you."

"But it *was* me," Eaon insisted, a light smile dimpling his cheeks. "It was the most *me* I've felt in a long time. His cousin keeps these salamanders in cages, and we were drunk on whiskey, and I was complaining how much I hated seeing animals in cages, because we don't do that here, you know. It's barbaric."

Eaon was getting wound up, his words coming too fast the way they did sometimes when he was in a frenzy. Dearmead listened to every word, taking in the animated way Eaon talked with his hands, his face beaming.

"So Tomaii, it was his idea, he's kind of wild, he said something and then the next thing I knew we were sneaking through the gorge to go and free them. It was . . . I got in so much trouble for that later. But we let them loose and then ran all the way to the bottom of the gorge to hide, because, oh I forgot to tell you, they're Igni-blessed, so Reigan was chasing us with a flint, threatening to light us both on fire. We hid in the iridescent flower farm at the bottom of the gorge, and . . . it was beautiful.

"Tomaii isn't afraid of anything. And he made me unafraid, too. Mother of all, why didn't you tell me how good it feels, Dea? To be touched like that? It wasn't like how I thought it would be. It didn't feel like I was giving up my body to be useful. He wanted to make *me* feel good, and oh, it was so good."

His eyes unfocused again as Eaon took a shallow breath, pulling his bottom lip between his teeth.

"Wait, what are you talking about? Did you have sex?" Dearmead felt his temperature rising, a tightness in his chest.

Eaon thought Dearmead knew how it felt, but he didn't. He was imagining it now, though. What it would be like to be touched. To touch. His eyes were fixated on the way Eaon's lip reddened as he held onto it with his teeth, the rise and fall of his chest beneath the linen shirt that hung too loosely around his collarbones, worn and stretched.

Something hot and bitter in his throat made Dearmead wrinkle his nose.

Eaon smirked and hit Dearmead's shoulder with the back of his hand. "Get your jealousy off your face before Celeste freezes it like that."

Dearmead scoffed and rolled his eyes, but the burning inside got worse. Eaon was joking, but that word . . . it was what this feeling was. Dearmead was jealous. Eaon had been with a male, and Dearmead was jealous.

***

There were ten hours between when Dearmead said goodbye to Eaon for the day and when they met at the waterfall again the next morning, but that was all the time it took for Eaon's family to have stolen his smile. He arrived in the cave with a split lip and dark shadows under his tired eyes.

"What happened?" Dearmead demanded as he stood, staff clutched in his hand.

"Same shit as always," Eaon spat, pacing back and forth. "I don't want to talk about it. What are we doing today?"

Dearmead watched Eaon pace for a moment. Watched his

fists clench and unclench, his upper lip twitch in a hidden sneer, the quick jerk of his chin to one side as he wrestled with whatever it was festering inside.

"Tell me who it was and I'll— "

"It's not worth it. They'll die soon anyway."

Dearmead raised an eyebrow, but Eaon didn't notice as he stopped moving. Closing his eyes, rocking back and forward on his heels, his lips moved as if he were talking but no sound came out.

Slowly, Dearmead put his staff down and took a few silent steps until he was close enough to take Eaon's elbow. "Hey."

"All the lines are blurry."

"Okay. Come and sit. I brought some lychees."

He'd brought a whole basket of snacks, not liking how the weeks away from the Boab left Eaon weaker. Blinking away whatever haze had descended over his mind, Eaon let Dearmead take him to the back of the cave to sit down.

"Eat. I have to do magic today and I don't want you passing out."

"Magic?"

"Yeah," Dearmead said with a grimace, reaching for his staff again. "Some of the marks on my staff have worn off and I have to redo them."

From the second basket Dearmead had brought, he selected a long knife made of granite and began sharpening the edge. For a long while, they sat in silence, Eaon feasting on fruits and eggs while Dearmead traced fresh marks. Every now and then he would mutter a spell, offering his intentions to Terra, who let his magic flow freely. The staff strengthened in his hand until he wasn't sure which was harder, the granite or the wood.

"You're really going through with it then?" Eaon asked quietly, sounding more like himself.

"Through with what?"

"Being a guardian."

Dearmead picked a splinter out of his thumb with his teeth, keeping his eyes locked on the sun filtering gently through the wall of water.

"It's far too late to change my mind now. A few more years and I'll graduate." He wasn't sure why he added, "There's honor in being a guardian."

"There's honor in being a scout, too."

"There's honor in respecting my family's wishes."

Not just his ma, who his resentment for grew with every passing word, but for the rest of the Bayfield guardians who had grown to respect him.

Eaon pondered over the mango pip between his fingers, twisting his mouth before wincing at the way it pulled at the wound splitting his lip. "There is strength in forging your own path."

They would argue about this all day if Dearmead let them.

"Didn't you hear your da yesterday? Guardians might have to go with travelers soon, and you won't need me to be a scout."

Eaon rolled his eyes and sucked the pip clean before wrapping it in a scrap of cloth, probably to give to his ma later to powder. Why was it only now that Dearmead was noticing how long Eaon's fingers were? How he drummed them mindlessly on the ground as he leaned back against the wall and stared at the waterfall. The way the cord of muscle down his neck twinged as his jaw clenched and released, a bad mood settling in. Looking at his face, Dearmead longed to see one of Eaon's slow, wide smiles that would mask his silent laughter until it built and overflowed into something he couldn't contain.

"It isn't like this in the North Mountains."

Dearmead turned back to his staff, pressing the blade in harder than strictly necessary. "No?"

"People choose their roles. Whatever they want."

"What about the jobs that nobody wants to do?"

"The ones that have to be done? They take turns doing them."

"Relying on the goodwill of others to keep it fair?" Dearmead raised his brows again, skeptical.

"Better than selling yourself for scraps," Eaon muttered. "Better than bleeding in the hope of mercy from people who hate you."

Despite the strength of the wood in his hands, Dearmead nearly snapped the staff in two.

"Couldn't Eavha or your ma heal your face?"

"Eavha's going through a phase. And ma hasn't seen it yet."

"What phase?"

"An I'm-better-than-everyone-and-enjoy-watching-people-worship-the-ground-I-walk-on phase," Eaon snorted.

Glancing to where he was working, Eaon took the knife and inspected the edge of it. Seeing him with a blade, knowing what kind of mood he was in, made Dearmead more nervous than he had been in a while. But Eaon picked up the sharpening stone and passed it over the edge.

Dearmead shook his head. "She's going to grow up to be a bitch."

"She's sixteen. And she *is* better than everyone else."

"Magic and talent doesn't equal better."

Eaon scoffed, but the sharp edge of his words had softened once again. "Dea, you might be the only witch in Wyldeden who thinks that."

# CHAPTER 13

# WANTING

For the entire following year, every time Eaon went traveling he returned with a new story about another male. It was worse when he wasn't in one of his moods, because Dearmead knew it hadn't been impulsive. Eaon would blush as he talked about them, hiding little smiles and trailing his fingers down his shins, as if remembering the touch.

Allarin from the western sands, who'd taught Eaon all the dirtiest Kervish phrases. Nicolaz from the far-eastern port city in Hyrsch, who'd seduced him with song and tasted like olives. And now Mustavrick from the southern mountains, who'd shown Eaon the incandescent crystal caves beneath the frozen wastes before getting on his knees.

Dearmead knew he was wasn't being fair as he sat beneath a peeling paperbark tree, boiling beneath his skin, a headache crawling up the sides of his temples as he ground his teeth together. Knew it, but was unable to control it.

He sighed.

Loudly.

Eaon stopped talking midsentence and blinked at him, tucking his hands under his arms. "Sorry. I'm talking too much."

"No," Dearmead said urgently, leaning forward on his knees. "Not at all. I love your stories."

They sat by the river below the waterfalls again, the peppercorn scent of the surrounding bush and the soft white and green flora that sprinkled the ground familiar and soothing. Bright sunlight filtered through the sparse canopy, letting Eaon soak in it after spending so long below ground on the other side of the spine. His skin had paled a little, the warmth of him dulled.

"Then, what?" Eaon asked as his brows pulled together.

"What?"

"You know what. I know you. So just say it."

Dearmead looked away and picked a blade of grass, twisting and shredding it. As the loud silence lingered, Eaon waited patiently. The exact words Dearmead wanted eluded him, wouldn't make a coherent sentence in his head, but his mouth started moving anyway.

"Just . . . I don't want to hear about how you fucked some witch in a crystal cave in the Southern Spine, okay?"

Eaon flinched, pulling one knee up under his chin. The color creeping up his neck was a different kind of blush. "Sorry. I didn't mean to make you uncomfortable."

"I'm not," Dearmead amended, berating himself silently. "I like hearing about your trips more than anything. But I'm sick of hearing about you throwing yourself at any guy who gives you attention."

Eaon's face became very still, his shoulders curling in. Dearmead's body was trembling with the things he was close to saying, but he held his tongue as he saw the pain he'd caused. Forced his brain to put together the right words.

"I just meant, you deserve better."

Quietly, Eaon mumbled, "There is nothing better for someone like me."

"Eaon, that's—"

"No, Dearmead, go rogue." In the space of a heartbeat, Eaon's shame twisted to fury, glaring spitefully at the shadow of their cave behind the periwinkle fall. "I'm not like you, remember? I won't ever have a future with someone here, because who the fuck would want to be with a useless piece of shit like me? So I'm sorry if my taking a little affection where I can get it offends you, because there sure as shit isn't anything for me in this fucking cage, and—"

Dearmead couldn't stand it. Couldn't listen to Eaon talk about himself like that anymore. Leaning over, he took his face and kissed him. Sweetly. The way he had imagined doing for months.

"There's me," he said, pulling back, hands trembling.

Eaon blinked, fingers hovering over his lips in stunned stillness.

For longer than Dearmead could stand, Eaon just stared at him as if he had, until this moment, been entirely unaware of the effect he had over him. Oblivious to the way Dearmead watched enviously as he spoke of his encounters with the other witches, the heat that brewed under his skin.

But he was seeing it now. Eaon's fingers trailed from his lip to his chin as he noticed the restraint in Dearmead's breathing. The tautness of him as he tried to keep still, letting Eaon adjust to the idea of him. Of them.

"You?" The word was a breath on the wind, but the amber in his eyes was burning.

Dearmead nodded, and that was all it took for his self-control to crumble. He took Eaon's face in one palm again. "Me."

"You."

Then Eaon leaned in.

His eyes shuttered and Dearmead met him half way. This time Eaon kissed him back, strong and sure. Urgent, even, as he opened wider, sneaking in a breath as his tongue pressed against Dearmead's mouth. Following Eaon's lead, Dearmead mirrored the movement, letting Eaon in deeper, harder. Every fiber of his being wanted to be closer, his hand sliding up the back of Eaon's neck.

The touch seemed to spark something in Eaon. He moved, pushing against Dearmead until his back was against the paperbark trunk, swinging one leg over his lap, hands pressed against Dearmead's chest.

This wasn't a dream. He didn't have the imagination to conjure up the heat of Eaon's mouth on his, the weight of him on his lap. The fire that flooded his veins as Eaon pulled his shirt off and flung it aside. Everything else ceased to exist, Dearmead's body straining inside the leather.

"Touch me," Eaon begged as he broke the kiss.

Unable to be away from of him, Dearmead kissed Eaon's neck, moaning at the taste of his skin. Eaon shuddered at the sound of it, but as Dearmead's fingers brushed down his sides, Eaon stilled. The rapid rise and fall of his chest against Dearmead's was slowing.

"What's wrong?" Dearmead murmured into his neck. When Eaon didn't answer, he looked up. "Eaon?"

He had his eyes closed, taking deep measured breaths.

"Eaon."

"No."

Dearmead frowned, reaching for his face again until Eaon flinched back.

"No. No."

He was pushing back before he opened his eyes.

"Did I do something?" Dearmead asked, holding onto the trunk as he stood.

Eaon ignored him as he went to collect his shirt, padding back into the bordering forest.

Of course, Dearmead followed. "Eaon, if I did something to upset you, tell me. I didn't mean to. I've never done this before, so—"

Eaon whined, shaking his head as he pulled his shirt back on. "No, it's not you. I'm sorry. This just isn't a good idea."

Dearmead stopped himself from asking why. Stopped following him.

Eaon was flustered, panicked, practically breaking into a run. *Escaping*, was the word that came to mind.

And it was only that word that made him realize why. He hadn't thought of it until now because, well, he didn't tend to think of these things. Especially not when it came to Eaon. His friend, who didn't have the luxury of not thinking about the dynamic between them. That Dearmead was a Wyldeden guardian and Eaon was a laborer.

It didn't matter to Dearmead, not at any level. It never had. But Eaon had almost been forced to do these things with people who treated him like shit, people who outranked him, so maybe it mattered to him. Maybe the reason he had never looked at Dearmead that way before, the reason he only looked for affection from males outside the Boab, was because nobody out there had ever tried to abuse him that way.

Hissing, Dearmead grabbed his staff and hit the closest

paperback tree. One day he would find out who'd been involved and cave their fucking heads in. But for now, he'd give Eaon some space. Later, he'd apologize. Eaon deserved better than the casual flings he found out in Nir, but he deserved better than a reminder of what almost happened to him, too.

# CHAPTER 14
# HAPPINESS

For the first time in Eaon's twenty-one years of life, his head was completely silent. There was only panic making his blood course coldly through his body as he stomped through the forest, grief making every step heavier, and the warmth lingering on his lips. Lips he had not been able to stop touching since the moment Dearmead had kissed them.

*"There's me."*

No, there wasn't.

Stopping, Eaon looked around the birch trees for signs that Dearmead was following him. Only the twittering of birds and the far away call of an angry possum met him. Good. That was good. But without the cave, he didn't know where else he could go where nobody would find him. Going home was not an option, at least until his ma finished at the clinic. The new Head of House had something to prove and Eaon made a point to stay as far away as possible until he and Kailevi could leave again.

Turning to one of the trees, Eaon found a foothold and hauled himself up the trunk, creeping along the branches until he found a sturdy one to lounge on with enough foliage to hide him from any passersby.

Again, his fingers pressed against his mouth.

*"You deserve better."*

*"There's me."*

There couldn't be.

The moment passed through his mind again as the annoyance lining Dearmead's face took on new meaning. With all the time Eaon spent away, he had assumed Dearmead made other friends. That his annoyance and distraction came from thinking about all the other things he'd rather be doing than listening to Eaon. All the people he'd rather be around. That the time they spent together was from habit, from some kind of pity lingering in the kindness that existed in Dearmead despite Calla's best efforts.

Eaon had done nothing to deserve it.

*"There's me."*

There shouldn't be.

Dearmead's future was full of possibility. The whispers that had begun in their secondary education classes as Dearmead had come into himself, filling out like the guardian-in-training he was, had only gotten louder as they moved into tertiary. Everybody looked at Dearmead, either with jealousy or longing. Even Eavha blushed and stuttered stupidly whenever she and Dearmead were in a room together.

And why wouldn't they? He was all broad shoulders and hard muscle. That hair, especially when free of its braid, glistened like a sheet of obsidian down to his taut waist, screaming to have hands running through it. Quiet and broody, yet unabashedly kind at the same time. He had a moral compass no Bayfield had any business having.

And he had absolutely no business wasting himself on

someone like Eaon. Someone without roots, without spine, without a damned thing to offer. He would float from place to place for the rest of his life, utterly useless.

"Stupid," Eaon spat, wishing he had stayed to smack Dearmead up the back of his head.

It wasn't as if they could be together the way Eaon was with other males. Brief, temporary encounters. Meaningless moments of passion that, at least while it lasted, made Eaon feel wanted. No, Dearmead thought Eaon deserved better. Thought that he would be better. It would not be some fleeting carnal balm to ease the ache that had settled deep into Eaon's heart.

He had to find him. Tell him he was stupid, and try to salvage some kind of friendship. It was the right thing to do.

So why was his throat tight, his breaths shallow and strained?

* * *

Once he was sure his ma would be home, Eaon snuck through the door to their private kitchenette. Eavha was sitting at the table wrapping loose hairs around a daisy while his ma ground sunflower seeds into a fine powder.

"Somebody's in trouble," Eavha sang, smirking at Eaon as he closed the door.

"No, you're not," Ellissa said, turning in her chair to smile warmly. "The Head was asking after you, but I told them you were running errands for me."

"Oh, thanks. Sorry," Eaon muttered, running a hand through his hair.

"Are you alright?"

"Yes, I just . . ."

He didn't want to talk about it, but as his fingers

subconsciously found their way back to his lips again, Eavha's smirk turned feral.

"Oh, Mother bear witness, Eaon's been kissed! Who's your girlfriend?"

Heat bloomed across his face. "Go rogue, you brat."

Eavha flinched. "Ma!"

"Eaon," Ellissa warned him, but there was something bright in her eyes that made his stomach flip around. "Sit."

"I'm tired."

"Sit."

There would be no escaping. With a sigh, he took the other seat beside her and stuck his tongue out at Eavha's smug face. Tutting, Eavha let her magic swell until Eaon's vision began to blur.

"Careful or I'll hex you so you can't stick it back in."

Ellissa slammed a hand down on the table. "You will do no such thing. Go somewhere else."

The magic fell flat and Eavha flicked her hair over her shoulder as she stood, giving Eaon one last arrogant smirk.

"She's so annoying," Eaon hissed.

"You'll get your vengeance one day," Ellissa chuckled, then lay a hand over the one Eaon left resting on the table. "But she was right, wasn't she? Tell me."

"Ma, no. It's . . . It's not worth talking about. Nothing's going to come of it. It was a mistake."

Ellissa narrowed her eyes. "Did she say that?"

Eaon didn't answer. Doing so would only invite further conversation about a long list of things he did not want to be talking to his mother about.

"Did *he* say that?"

Eaon stiffened.

"Your da and I talk, you know."

"I'm going to my room."

Eaon stood, but Ellissa clutched his hand.

"I know what you're going to say," he said as she opened her mouth to speak.

"I highly doubt that."

"You want me to be happy, but our family is dying and you need me to breed."

"No."

"Good, because I doubt my genetics are something worth passing on to some poor witchling anyway."

"Eaon, stop it."

Eaon remained stoic as he looked out the window. He didn't want to see his mother's disappointment. Or her pity. Or her worry.

"Your da needs to head out again already, and I assume you'll want to go with him."

Eaon snapped his head around. "So soon?"

Ellissa nodded, petting Eaon's hand. "Take this time to figure out what it is that you want."

He didn't understand the heaviness in her voice. "What do you mean?"

"You haven't been given a lot of choices in your life, and I'm sorry for that. But this . . ." She reached over to place a hand over Eaon's staccato heart. "You get to follow this."

The words didn't hit the way he knew she wanted them to.

"It's not that simple."

"It is."

"Ma, maybe for you, or for Eavha, but me—"

"I will do whatever I have to so that it is that simple for you, too." This time her promise hit home, and Eaon's eyes welled up against his will as she continued. "You have always done what you have to. What your da and I have asked you to do for

Eavha's sake. Don't think we don't know the toll it takes. We see you, Eaon, and I will burn this family to the ground to give you an iota of happiness."

Eaon pulled his hand away to tuck them beneath his arms, turning to stare at the daisy chains strung across the ceiling. Not for the first time, Eaon wondered if his ma had placed a curse on her own family as revenge for what they had done to him, but that didn't make any sense. The rapid decline in their family's numbers had begun long before Eaon was even born. Though during the worst of the nights when he lay awake in bed, terrified someone would come into his room to drag him away for the laborer "training" he had never undertaken, he liked to imagine his mother loved him enough to do something so violent and cruel.

"Whoever it is, whoever you *choose*, Eaon," Ellissa continued, shifting her chair closer until her presence was undeniable. "They would be lucky to have you in their life."

The dam broke, and though he couldn't find the words to express it, Eaon looked to his ma as the pain of it spilled over.

"I know," she whispered, amber eyes glistening as she took both his hands again and pulled him close. Wrapping her arms around him, Eaon devolved into a twelve-year-old witchling again, sobbing in his mother's arms after being stood on, his face pushed into a splinter-ridden rug.

CHAPTER 15

# WAITING

Dearmead made his ma proud that evening as he trained with his brothers, hitting hard enough to draw blood. It was his own face he imagined as he knocked Trumard down, swinging the practice staff with every intention of caving in his skull.

The Mother had forgotten to add some fucking sense when she'd made Dearmead; for the life of him, he couldn't remember what had made him think kissing Eaon was a good idea. All year he had listened to the exciting adventures Eaon had been on, seen the way he came alive talking about Nir before the reality of Wyldeden turned him back into a shell. Of all the males in all of Nir, why would Eaon want to be stuck with someone bound to the Boab. Why would he want the drama of someone too spineless to stand up to his savage ma, who grinned gleefully as Trumard tapped out of the fight.

"What is wrong with you? You could have killed me," Trumard spat as he rolled to his feet, blood dripping down his chin.

"If he had, it would have been your own fault," Calla sneered, squeezing Dearmead's shoulder.

Shrugging her off, Dearmead tossed his practice staff to the ground.

"I'm going for a walk."

"Sit with me at dinner," Calla called after him before picking up the staff and turning to her other son. "Trumard. Second stance. Now."

Wincing, Dearmead felt slightly guilty for leaving his older brother to endure a beating. There was no winning against her, and she didn't allow her children to tap out.

But there would be no calm, no rest, until he apologized to Eaon.

<hr>

Knocking on the Nemuse's kitchen door, the one directly attached to Kailevi and Ellissa's wing of the manor, Dearmead checked that the pastries he'd brought were still intact. Raspberry cream—Eaon's favorite.

Eavha opened the door and beamed up at him, tucking one of her unruly curls behind her ears.

"Hi Dea."

"Hey Eavha. Is Eaon home?"

"He already left."

Dearmead looked toward the forest. Talking in the cave might be a better idea anyway.

"With da," Eavha clarified.

Before he could drop the pastries, his heart seizing, the door was pulled all the way open.

"Dearmead?" Ellissa tilted her head, looking him over curiously.

"Sorry, ma'am," Dearmead bowed deeply. "I didn't mean to interrupt your evening."

"Not at all, why don't you come in."

"I was actually just looking for Eaon, but,"—the words choked him, face going numb— "he left."

Ellissa looked from Dearmead's slouching shoulders to the pastries in his hand and smiled. "Come in. He thought you might come by and left some things to pass on to you."

"Are they passionfruit?" Eavha asked, taking the pastries and peeking under the canvas lid. "Ugh. They'll do. Next time bring passionfruit."

"Noted," Dearmead said absently as he stepped inside.

Ellissa walked to the little table Eaon ate at with Kailevi, two books and a letter tied into a little package with twine sitting there.

"He said you'd want to read these. And this is still sealed," Ellissa said, handing him the pile. Then she tutted at Eavha and shooed her from the bench where she'd put the pastries. "They're not for you."

"They won't be any good by the time Eaon gets back."

Dearmead sat and checked the titles of the books Eaon had picked out for him first. One was fiction, a human story about spies and politics that promised to keep him awake all night. The second was closer to Eaon's speed, something academic that Dearmead would usually scoff at. Later, he would go to the library and borrow a dictionary so he could scour every word.

Finally, he broke the wax seal on the letter. Eaon had never written him a letter. There was no need, since whispering leaves were faster and more discreet.

*'Wait for me. Please. I have too much to say.'*

Dearmead traced every line of Eaon's tidy, looping inscription. He would wait. Gladly.

# CHAPTER 16
# SECRET

Fourteen months later, Dearmead was still waiting.

Gossip speculated that the Nemuse duo had died, sparking a resurgence from the other travelers for Kailevi's petition to be heard. There hadn't even been a whispering leaf to explain their prolonged absence, but nobody was sent to look for them, and the petition went to the bottom of the high priestess's large stack of paperwork.

"They'll be back any day," Ellissa said whenever Dearmead stopped by to check on them. The senior healer kept her chin high, ignoring the whispers from what little was left of the rest of the Nemuses. Their gratitude that the Lover had finally taken them, and relief that neither could pass on whatever gene they had that Terra and Sanni had turned their noses at.

Even Eavha had quietened, spending most of her free time at the temples praying for her da and brother's safe return. Dearmead joined her as often as he could.

He couldn't sleep. Could barely stomach his food. Trumard

got his revenge over and over as the stress of it took its toll on his concentration.

"Still worrying about that useless floor-scrubber you're so obsessed with?" Trumard teased, standing over where Dearmead had landed on his back, black spots still dancing across his vision from the blow.

"Go rogue."

"You should hear ma singing her praises to the Lover about it."

Dearmead kicked up into Trumard's balls with enough force that he wasn't sure his brother would ever breed. As he vomited on the lawn, Dearmead got up and stormed from the property toward the city.

All Eaon's stories about the beasts that roamed the forests ran on repeat through his mind. Even if whatever illness the Nemuse line was falling to hadn't reached Eaon yet, there were so many other things out there that could kill him. Dearmead didn't even know what season it was meant to be out there. What if he'd gone south during the winter again and frozen to death? Or starved? What if one of the slavers had mistaken them for demi-kin and taken them to one of the human cities? Eaon had no magic to prove he wasn't, and even so, scouts had heard rumors that the royals took low-blessed rogues or wild witches as slaves too.

He had read the two books Eaon left for him back to front so many times he could recite them from memory, the letter Eaon had left almost falling apart from how many times Dearmead had opened and closed it. He almost couldn't remember exactly what Eaon would sound like saying the words anymore.

The realization stole the breath from his lungs.

He stopped at the crest of a hill, as he did every day, and

looked toward the Great Boab on its island in the middle of the lake.

"I'm waiting," he whispered.

As if it heard him, the crease in the fold where the witchmark lay widened.

He'd know the shape of Eaon anywhere.

The entire settlement disappeared as Dearmead ran. He didn't remember how he got to the lake so quickly, but when Eaon spotted him, pale and shaken, he ran to meet him.

Who pulled who in, it didn't matter. They held each other for a long minute, the relief weakening his knees. Only the fact that Eaon was literally shaking kept him standing.

"What happened?"

"Rogues," Eaon muttered.

"Here?"

Eaon shook his head, pulling back.

Kailevi had finished crossing the bridge, nodding his greeting to Dearmead with a tired, solemn expression.

"Go," he told Eaon. "I need to see your ma. She'll be worried sick."

Eaon took off his pack and let Kailevi take it, then grabbed Dearmead's hand and led the way to the waterfall. He wasn't as thin as Dearmead feared, though filthy and battered, strands of blood-soaked hair grown down to his shoulders.

When they reached the water, Eaon stopped, breathing raggedly as he stared at the perfect glittering surface. Dearmead waited for him to let go of his hand, but Eaon held on tight.

"Are you alright?" Dearmead asked quietly.

Eaon didn't answer for a moment, eyes wide. There was a pale scar under his eyebrow, light enough to go unnoticed by anyone who didn't know the dips and planes of his face intimately.

He loosed a shaky breath. "I thought I was going to die."

Dearmead's heart caught in his throat. Before he could stop himself, he was stepping closer, wanting to pull him close.

"And the only thing that scared me about that was that I might never get to see you again. Never apologize for walking away from you."

"You don't have to apologize." Dearmead squeezed Eaon's hand. "And you're home now. It's safe here."

Eaon grimaced, and Dearmead knew what he was thinking. Knew Eaon would still rather go back out into Nir with the rogues than stay here for too long with what was left of his family.

"Do you want to talk about it?" he offered.

Eaon shook his head. "Not yet."

So they stood watching the waterfall until Eaon's knees finally gave out. Then Dearmead helped him into the water, carefully pulling the stale rag of a shirt from Eaon's bruised body. Another scar, still pink and shiny, curled around his shoulder blade, and Eaon flinched as Dearmead ran his finger along it.

"Not yet," Eaon croaked, sinking deeper into water that clouded with dirt and blood.

"I'll wait," Dearmead promised, holding onto Eaon's arm to keep him steady. With his other hand, he stroked back Eaon's hair, rubbing the filth out of the mats. "As long as you need."

The words drew up Eaon's haunted gaze.

"I dreamed that you didn't. And I was glad."

Dearmead kept his face pointedly neutral as he continued to help Eaon clean his hair.

"We don't have to talk about it right now."

Gripping Dearmead's forearm, Eaon pulled himself upright. He didn't speak right away, whatever horrors he'd seen the past year still trying to make space for Eaon to come back to himself.

"That day . . . when you kissed me." Eaon swallowed, closing his eyes as if that was almost as hard to remember as the rogues. "You can't, Dearmead. Your ma would kill you for being with someone like me. It's bad enough to bring shame to my own family, but to let you bring it to yours—"

"I don't care what she thinks. I don't care how much magic you have. I like you, Eaon. I have for a long time."

There it was. Finally, he'd said the words that had been stuck in his throat for years. Rather than feel better, Dearmead was just nauseous.

Eaon drew his lip between his teeth before opening his eyes, but he still couldn't look at him. When he didn't say anything, Dearmead said it for him.

"You like me too. I know you do."

Eaon nodded.

"I can handle Ma."

"I don't want you to have to."

"So we keep it a secret for a while. Until I can make her see how amazing you are."

"Dea." Eaon's skepticism was palpable.

Dearmead cupped Eaon's face the way he had dreamed of doing since the day he'd left. The rush of it left him dizzy, words disintegrating into meaningless sounds. But he had to speak. He had to tell Eaon.

"You are. You're amazing. You're the smartest witch I've ever met. You speak twelve languages and tell amazing stories. You're funny and exciting and beautiful, so beautiful, Mother knows I can barely stop looking at you. I hate every minute we don't spend together. It shouldn't matter how blessed you are because you make me happy, and I want to make you happy."

Eaon had closed his eyes again, flinching at every compliment.

Dearmead let a shaking hand slip down his neck, stepping through the water until he could put his forehead against Eaon's.

"I want to tell you every day how incredible you are until you start believing me."

Eaon moved. As his lips pressed against Dearmead's, heat bloomed through his face, his mouth parting instantly to let Eaon in. Hands trembling, he tightened his grip on Eaon to stop him from running away again.

But Eaon wasn't running.

Desperately, as if clinging to life itself, Eaon threaded his fingers beneath the buckles of Dearmead's leather, pressing in closer until there was no space, no air. Which was okay, because this was all they needed.

Eaon pulled away first, panting into the crook of Dearmead's neck. "You want to go to the cave?"

Dearmead glanced over Eaon's shoulder to the waterfall. The shadow behind it where the two of them had been together in every way except this.

"Eaon, listen, don't laugh at me." He didn't know why he bothered to say it. Eaon had never laughed at him. "I've never done this before."

"Oh." His hand released Dearmead's buckles, tenderly taking his braid and wrapping it around his fist. "We don't have to."

"I want to."

Eaon lifted his gaze to assess Dearmead's face, but he wouldn't find any hesitation.

"I'll take care of you. I promise."

Dearmead kissed him again. A gentle, sweet thing that was

rapidly devolving into the kind of carnal need Eaon had described so clearly. A part of him couldn't believe this was actually happening. But it was. The heat, the pressure, the solidity of Eaon's body holding onto him wasn't something Dearmead had the ability to imagine. When he pulled back again, Dearmead's next words were meant in every possible way.

"We'll take care of each other."

# About the Author

 Alex Clifford is an emerging author from the coffee capital: Melbourne, Australia. They have spent the past decade studying creative writing, interior design, sociology, psychology, and secondary education. As a neurodiverse, queer, widowed, single parent, Alex is excited to bring their unique perspective to the fantasy genre for many years to come. For more on Alex Clifford's upcoming work, visit: www.alexclifford.com.au

You can find them on social media at:
Facebook: facebook.com/AfsCliffordBooks
Twitter: @AfsClifford
Instagram: @almost_alex
TikTok: @alexcliffordwrites

www.ingramcontent.com/pod-product-compliance
Lightning Source LLC
Chambersburg PA
CBHW020228120726
47903CB00008B/2583